WILD HORSE CREEK 4

Desert Rescue

SHARON SIAMON

Desert Rescue

WILD HORSE CREEK 4 Desert Rescue
Copyright: Text copyright © Sharon Siamon 2010
The author asserts her moral right to be identified as the author of
the work in relation to all such rights as are granted by the author
to the publisher under the terms and conditions of this agreement.
Original title: Desert Rescue
Cover and inside illustrations: © 2010 Jennifer Bell
Cover layout: Stabenfeldt AS

Typeset by Roberta L. Melzl
Editor: Bobbie Chase
Printed in Germany, 2010

ISBN: 978-1-934983-59-1

Stabenfeldt, Inc.
225 Park Avenue South
New York, NY 10003
www.pony.us

Available exclusively through PONY.

Contents

CHAPTER 1
First Look

Liv Winchester had wandered away from her twin sister, Sophie. She stood perfectly still, staring at a poster on the airport wall. The picture showed a girl on a black horse. It was just a "Welcome to Arizona" poster, but it summed up all the longing Liv felt inside.

She could be that girl – if only they would stay long enough on the Lucky Star ranch to capture and tame the wild black stallion. She'd seen him twice near the ranch. In her mind she could see him right now, running free across the desert, beautiful, powerful, free!

"Liv. Come on! The plane from Vancouver just landed." Sophie, her heart-shaped face framed in a halo of fine dark hair, grabbed her sister's hand and dragged her away. "I can't wait to see Mark!"

They sped through the crowd to their mother, Jess,

who was watching the passengers appear through a doorway one by one.

We've all missed my smart, funny brother, Liv thought. *Especially Sophie. She hates changes.* When their parents had split and Mark had gone to live with their father, Sophie had felt it most. Now she hoped they'd be a family again, living on the Lucky Star ranch with Gran and Granddad.

"Do you think he'll look different?" Sophie asked, dancing from one foot to the other anxiously.

"We saw him in April." Liv laughed. "How different could he look in four months?"

"Well, you've changed. Your hair is a lot longer and thicker, and it's got blonde streaks from the sun. And you look ... taller," Sophie said. They weren't identical twins. Sophie was smaller and slighter.

Liv hoped she wouldn't keep growing until she was taller than everybody else her age. Other than that, she loved the way she'd changed since they'd come to her grandparents' ranch. It was more than the way she looked, the way the sun had streaked her brown hair gold. Riding across the wide-open desert on her horse, Cactus Jack, had strengthened her whole body. And the black mystery stallion had given her a dream. If only they could stay ... if only Mark would love the ranch as much as she did!

"Here he comes!" their mother shouted. "Oh, Mark!"

Liv and Sophie froze. The tall young man slouching

toward them couldn't be their big brother. He wore a hooded sweatshirt that completely hid his eyes and face. His baggy pants hung low and his shoes flopped on his feet. His knapsack hung on one thin shoulder. A phone was clutched to his ear.

He barely looked up as his mother flung her arms around him.

Liv and Sophie exchanged one shocked glance and hurried to join them. It wasn't so much that Mark's clothes were different. It was the way he wore them, as if he had shrunk inside.

"Hey, Mark," Liv said softly.

"We're so glad to see you," Sophie gulped.

"Hey, little sisters." Mark stepped away from his mother and stuffed the phone in his pocket. A crooked grin lit his face for a second, then disappeared.

"We'll wait here for your suitcase," Jess told Mark as he turned to walk away.

"Everything I've got is in here." He patted his knapsack. "I'm not staying long, am I?"

Liv and Sophie exchanged another startled look.

"You won't need much." Sophie cleared her throat. "Maybe something cooler than that heavy sweatshirt. It's really hot outside." She pointed to the palm trees outside the airport window.

"We can get you a cowboy hat," Liv added quickly. "To protect … your head."

"I don't plan on being outside that much." Mark shrugged. "Which way to the van?"

"This way." His mother pointed to the exit. She hesitated. "I brought Granddad's truck, not the van."

Don't tell him we've sold the van! Sophie begged silently. Mark loved "the family bus," as Dad called it. Back in Vancouver he couldn't wait to get his license so he could drive it. But the van was useless on desert roads and Mom had needed the money. Mark would understand, once he saw the rough track to the Lucky Star ranch. Right now he looked on the brink of a meltdown. His face was pasty and his left eye was twitching. The sooner they got him home, the better.

"You're going to love Granddad's truck," Liv told him as she led the way to the exit. "You can drive it on the worst roads, or even out over the desert where there aren't any roads."

"An off-road vehicle." A shadow of Mark's smile reappeared. "Cool."

As they walked, he pulled his phone from his pocket. "Dad said to let him know when I got in," he told them, glancing at it, "...and it looks like I have a couple more messages."

He strode in front, head bowed, answering his text messages. Liv pulled Sophie back beside her. "What are we going to do?" she whispered.

"What do you mean?" Sophie's brown eyes widened.

11

"About Mark." Liv threw up her hands. "I think his head's shaved under that hood and he's wearing earrings. Can you imagine Granddad's face when he sees that?"

"I see what you mean," Sophie sighed. Their grandfather, Ted Starr, had a fierce way of looking at you – as if he was a hawk on a fencepost, and you were a mouse in his claws.

❋ ❋ ❋ ❋ ❋

"Welcome, son. Take off that hood you're wearin' and let me have a good look at my grandson," Granddad Starr thundered as Mark stepped out of the truck at the Lucky Star ranch.

"Go ahead, Mark," his mother urged.

Sophie could see Mark struggling against the urge to turn and run. He gazed, blinking, at the treeless ranch yard, the house, barn and horses in the corral. Sophie remembered how it felt when she'd first come. The desert had seemed so different from the tall trees and lush green of Vancouver. It had been hard to take a deep breath, as if the hot dry air would turn you to dust.

It's all right, she longed to tell her brother, *you'll get used to it.* Mark slowly peeled back the hood and unzipped his sweatshirt. *What would Granddad say?*

The sun beat down on Mark's shaved head and glittered off the gold ring in his ear. He squinted uncomfortably at his grandparents, Sandra and Ted Starr, waiting to greet him. From the veranda, bleached cow skulls with hollow eyes stared down at him as if they were sizing up the newcomer.

Granddad marched forward with his stiff stride. A big silver buckle at his waist matched his white hair and thick drooping moustache.

Mark backed up as if he expected to be hit. Granddad kept coming. He seized Mark's hand and shook it hard. "Welcome home," he croaked in his low, hoarse voice. "Come on in out of the sun and we'll get you a cool drink. Hand me that packsack of yours."

With a stunned expression on his pale face, Mark handed his grandfather his pack and followed him up the porch steps. Sophie, Liv, Gran and Jess trailed behind through the front door. The large ranch house living room had red Mexican tiles on the floor and dark wooden furniture. Light flooded in through windows set in thick stucco walls.

"Granddad hasn't said anything about Mark's earring," Liv hissed to Sophie.

Sophie whispered back, "Maybe he's so glad to see his only grandson he doesn't care how he looks. Or maybe he doesn't even notice the earring."

Their beaming grandmother was leading Mark off on a tour of the ranch house that had been in her family for generations. Gran was a slight, gray-haired woman with a straight back and brisk walk.

"I bet Shane will notice." Liv threw herself onto the couch in the ranch house living room.

"He might, but I'll bet he won't care, either," Sophie said. She'd had a crush on Shane Tripp since the moment the young cowboy rode into the ranch yard four months ago. He was sixteen, the same age as Mark, but the two of them couldn't look more different. "Shane said he was coming to meet Mark," Sophie sighed. "He should be here soon."

I'll have to remember not to show how much I like him, she reminded herself. *He thinks I'm too young for him*. Two years and ten months wasn't a huge age difference. But right now, it might as well be the distance to the moon.

CHAPTER 2
Granddad's Deal

It was almost five before they heard the clop of hooves coming across the ranch yard. Sophie burst out of the chair and raced for the door, Liv at her heels.

Shane was leaping off his buckskin paint horse Navajo as they ran up to him. He was as lean as an Arizona fence post, tall and wiry. His large cowboy hat, shirt, vest, jeans and boots suited him like a second skin. Beside him was his black and white border collie, Tux.

"Hope you don't mind. I brought Tux to dinner," Shane said, bending down to ruffle his dog's ears.

"Of course not!" Sophie knelt to kiss Tux on his black nose. "He's almost as much a member of the family as you."

Shane blushed as if the kiss had been for him.

"Our brother Mark's here." Sophie looked up at him. "He's ... he's ..."

"He's different than the way we described him." Liv stroked Navajo's soft tan and white nose.

Shane took Navajo's bridle off and loosened the saddle cinch. "I'll put my horse in the corral and be right in." He spoke in a quiet drawl. "I'm lookin' forward to meetin' Mark."

But as they all walked into the ranch house a few minutes later Liv and Sophie saw Shane's face freeze in surprise. It wasn't just the earrings. Mark was flopped in the depths of Ted Starr's favorite chair, eyes glued to a video game. He barely looked up long enough to say hello.

"Time for dinner," Gran announced from the dining room doorway. "Get your hands washed."

Mark's welcome home dinner was Mexican *burritos* filled with beef and beans, salad and delicious *tamales* wrapped in cornhusks. Gran was a fabulous cook, especially when it came to Mexican food.

All the talk around the table was about horses.

"The Lucky Star Spanish colonials came with your great-great-great grandmother from Mexico," Gran told Mark proudly. "They are descended from the original horses brought by the Spanish explorers."

"You saw them in the corral when you drove in," Liv said between mouthfuls of burritos. "Mine is the chestnut with the white blaze. His name is Cactus Jack." She didn't mention the wild black stallion. He was a Spanish colonial horse, too, but not part of the Lucky Star herd.

"Cactus Jack pulled Liv up a cliff when she slipped and fell in a storm,' Sophie added, her brown eyes shining. "He's amazingly strong. And smart."

"Sophie's horse, Cisco, is a sorrel." Liv handed Mark another *burrito*. "He's a great cow horse."

Sophie nodded eagerly. "Cisco turned away a stampede that was about to trample me! You should have seen it."

"We'll ride out tomorrow to see the whole Lucky Star herd," Granddad told Mark with a flourish of his fork. "My stallion Diego and his mares and foals are out along Wild Horse Creek. You'll see Spanish colonials the way they were meant to live – running free. We'll pick out one for you."

Mark kept his eyes firmly fixed on his plate. "I don't ride," he muttered. "I've never been on a horse. Riding's for girls."

"For girls!" Granddad exploded out of his chair. "Of all the … blamed nonsense!"

"It's all right, Granddad." Sophie put a smooth tanned hand on her Grandfather's arm. "Mark's never been on a horse. Wait till he sees you riding Diego, or Shane galloping Navajo across the range. He'll change his mind."

"Don't excite yourself, Ted," Gran warned. "Remember your heart."

Ted Starr sat back down, wiping his moustache with his napkin. "Which horse do you think Mark should ride, Shane?" he asked.

"I said, I don't ride." Mark stared down at his lap.

Ted Starr put down his fork. He sat straighter and his blue eyes blazed.

"You have to ride," Liv broke in. "There's no other way to get around out here on the ranch. No buses, no taxis and you can't ride a bike because the sand's too deep on the road."

"Then I'll stay here inside the house." Mark gestured around the low-ceilinged room. "It's cool."

There was a long pause. Neither Sophie nor Liv dared to look at Granddad.

"You could do that," he said at last. "But I'll make you a deal. You're sixteen. How'd you like to drive my truck?"

This made Mark look up. "I don't have a driver's license."

"Don't need one to drive around the ranch. I'll teach you to drive and help you get an Arizona license if you let Shane show you how to ride a horse. What do you say?"

Liv held her breath. Granddad's deal was an out-and-out bribe. Would it work? She watched Sophie cross her fingers hopefully. Something clattered to the floor. Mark's phone! He had been texting his friends under the table!

"All right," Mark muttered mutinously, bending over to retrieve his phone. "I'll get on a horse, but Liv and Sophie can teach me. I don't need lessons from a cowboy."

"Okay by me," Shane mumbled. Only Sophie noticed the hurt in his gray-blue eyes.

Liv was watching her grandfather. He was trying to hide it, but she knew how disappointed he must be in Mark at this moment. She was disappointed, and worried, too! What if Mark hated the ranch? What if he refused to stay? It could mean the end of all her dreams of living here and rescuing the black mystery stallion!

✳ ✳ ✳ ✳ ✳

That night, after Shane had gone, Liv and Sophie sat on the front veranda, feeling the night air draw the heat from the land, smelling the spicy scent of the mesquite trees and watching millions of stars sprinkled across the huge dome of the desert sky.

"I hope we can teach Mark to ride," Sophie sighed. "If we can't, Granddad's never going to let him drive the truck and he'll be miserable."

"I can teach him." Liv threw herself back in the big wooden porch chair. "Mark's a natural athlete. Remember him skiing at Whistler Mountain? The way he whizzed down the steepest trails?"

"That was last winter," Sophie reminded her. "He doesn't look very athletic now."

"It'll come back," Liv promised. "I just wish he didn't look so mad and weird all the time."

Sophie shrugged her slender shoulders. "It must have been tough living with Dad and that … that Elise person." She forced herself to say Dad's girlfriend's name.

"And, Mark was failing math and science." Liv stood

up and paced the veranda. "Do you know what our brother reminds me of?" She paused in her pacing and stared out into the desert night. "He reminds me of our black mystery stallion. He and Mark are both in places where they feel they don't belong, and people are pushing them around." She took a deep breath. "I wish I knew where that black horse is now."

"Probably causing trouble, wherever he is." Sophie looked up at her sister in the dim porch light. "Why do you want to find him? He fought with Diego and tried to run off with his mares. Then the next time we saw him he tore down the Heartbreak Hotel – with you inside!"

Liv paced again, her riding boots thumping down the porch boards. "That horse probably saved our lives wrecking the hotel. Yours, Shane's, mine – and Brady Bolt's." She went on, "If it hadn't been for the stallion, those horse smugglers would have caught us."

"That was the night you and Brady hooked up."

"I wouldn't say we 'hooked up'." Liv stared at the stars. "I like him, that's all. And I'm not sure how he feels about me. We were all so emotional that night …"

"I know what you mean!" Sophie shivered. The memory of being trapped in the hotel ballroom still haunted her. The wild horse had kicked and reared and stomped at the rotten beams of the crumbling hotel until the second floor came crashing down. Liv and Brady had all barely made it out alive. The last they'd seen of their mystery stallion was him chasing the smugglers down the dusty main street of a ghost town.

"I keep dreaming we'll see that horse again, and somehow tame him and make him ours," Liv said wistfully. "But I guess we never will."

"Not likely!" Sophie pulled herself up out of the deep veranda chair. "Hey, it's getting cold. I'm going in. Coming?"

"No," Liv said. "I want to plan Mark's riding lesson tomorrow. I'll take him out first thing in the morning while it's still cool. Cactus Jack will be a perfect lamb for Mark."

"I'll keep my fingers crossed." Sophie yawned. "Goodnight."

CHAPTER 3
Where's Our Mystery Stallion?

When everything was quiet, Liv went through the screen door and into Granddad's office. She switched on the computer and did a routine check of the horse rescue sites, the way she did almost every night. She was hoping there would be news of their mystery stallion.

With a jolt of hope, she enlarged a blurry photo of a recently rescued black stallion. Her toes tingled. It looked like this horse had a white blaze and four white socks – the right markings. *But this can't be our guy*, she thought, reading the description. *This wild horse comes from the Cerbat Mountains, up in northern Arizona. How would he get to a rescue station way down here?*

Liv knew that even if she could find *their* black stallion, the chances were slim she could adopt him.

He was probably too wild, too independent to ever tame. And what would they do with him here on the ranch? He'd already almost killed Diego. Granddad would never let them keep him.

Still, Liv knew she'd keep on checking this site, searching for her mystery horse. She scribbled the name of the rescue station – Gila Flats – on a piece of paper and stuffed it in her pocket. *I won't tell Sophie about this black horse I've seen,* Liv thought, as she turned off the computer. *He's probably not the same one and anyway, we have enough problems with Mark right now.*

✳ ✳ ✳ ✳ ✳

"Cactus Jack is ready for you," Liv told Mark as she led her chestnut horse into the cool dim barn. She put him in cross ties and went to get his grooming kit and saddle.

It was six-thirty the next morning and she'd had to drag her brother out of bed. He hung back against the barn wall, shoulders hunched, hands in his pockets.

Liv held out a curry comb to him. "Here, take this."

"What's that thing?" Mark scowled as he reached for the rubber grooming tool and turned it in his hands.

"It's a curry comb. Brush him down with it. Grooming is a good way to make friends with a horse."

Mark sidled closer. He had promised his grandfather he'd ride. If brushing the horse was part of it, he'd try. "Like this?" He dabbed at Cactus Jack's side.

"No, like this!" Liv brushed Cactus Jack's back and

sides with firm circular strokes. "You have to loosen all the dust in his coat. Now you do the other side."

Mark started to walk in a wide circle around Cactus Jack.

Liv yanked on his sleeve. "No, not like that! He could kick you into the next county! Walk close to his hind end. Put a hand on his back to let him know you're there. That way, if he kicks, he won't hurt you too bad."

"I don't want to get hurt at all," Mark said glumly. He watched Liv brush Cactus Jack down, pick up his feet and check his hooves for stones before she saddled and bridled him.

"You'll be doing all this yourself, soon," she promised.

"Don't bet on it," Mark snorted. "I'd be scared to pick up his feet like that."

"Don't show Cactus Jack you're scared," Liv advised. "He'll think there's something to be frightened of. Horses are very sensitive."

"Give me a car or a nice new pickup truck," Mark grumbled as Liv led Cactus Jack out to the corral and into the cool dawn of the desert. The sky above the hills to the east was a pale purple. Tall cactus spikes stood out against the dawn light. "With a truck you turn on the key and step on the gas," Mark went on. "It doesn't have feelings one way or the other about who's driving."

"But a horse is a living partner." Liv stroked Cactus Jack's smooth side, trying not to sound irritated. "It's not like driving some boring old machine!"

She could tell Mark wasn't convinced. When it came time to mount, he twisted backwards and forwards, trying to lift his foot high enough to fit in the stirrup. Finally, Cactus Jack just walked away. With one foot still in the air, Mark lost his balance and landed in the dust.

"I can't do it."

"Sure you can. It's like getting on a ski lift," Liv soothed. "Tricky the first time but easy once you get the feel of it."

Mark finally hoisted his left foot in the stirrup but when he tried to swing his leg over the horse's back he yanked so hard on the saddle it slipped sideways. Cactus Jack snorted and sidestepped. Mark thudded to the ground.

"This is hopeless," Mark groaned. "He doesn't want me up there."

"Try again," Liv urged. "I'll hold the saddle from the other side so it won't slip. You can do this."

But Jack's ears flattened his ears against his head when Mark approached. The whites of his eyes showed. He wasn't used to such a nervous, insecure rider. With a final hoist, Mark was in the saddle, perched on Cactus Jack like a kid on a riding toy. "Hold the reins just above his neck." Liv showed him. "Firm, but not too tight. Okay, now nudge him with your heels to make him go."

Mark hauled on the reins and kicked Cactus Jack's sides. "Giddiup!"

Cactus Jack, now totally confused, backed up and

spun in a circle. "Whoa, stop!" Mark shouted. "What is he doing?"

Liv could see Mark had stiffened into a knot of fear and tension. Cactus Jack must feel like he had a mountain lion on his back! "Don't yank on the reins," she yelled at Mark. "Sit back. Take a deep breath. Relax."

"RELAX?" screamed Mark. "Are you crazy? Why is he going in circles like this? Make him STOP!"

The scream was the last straw for Cactus Jack. He gave a sudden sideways hop. Mark flew off his back and landed with a hard thud in the corral sand. Cactus Jack trotted a few steps with his reins dangling, then stopped and looked back over his shoulder as if to say he was glad that was over.

Oh, my poor, hopeless brother. Liv's heart pounded as she ran to gather up Cactus Jack's loose reins. "Are you all right?" she called over her shoulder.

"Ow! Hey! What happened?" Mark slowly picked himself up, rubbing his hip.

With a shake of her head, Liv led Cactus Jack toward her brother. "You got tossed off, that's all. It could happen to anyone. Now you have to get right back on." She held out the reins to him.

"Are you kidding?" Mark waved away the reins. "I am never, do you hear me, Liv? Never getting on that horse again!"

CHAPTER 4
Mark's Misery

Mark turned to march out of the corral, then stopped with a groan. "Oh, no! Did everybody have to watch me make a fool of myself?"

Ranged along the corral fence, Liv saw that she and Mark had an audience. They hadn't noticed because they'd been concentrating so hard. Sophie and Gran looked sad, Shane embarrassed and Granddad angry.

"Climb back up there on Cactus Jack," Granddad hollered. "Otherwise you'll never ride again."

"That's my plan, Granddad." Mark put his head down, hunched his shoulders forward and stalked to the fence. He climbed awkwardly through the rails and headed for the ranch house. "Never riding again!" he shouted over his shoulder.

"I'll go talk to him." Sophie took off at a run. She caught up to Mark as he banged through the veranda door.

"Mom!" he yelled. "Where are you? I want to leave this stupid ranch and go home. Right now."

Sophie grabbed his arm and shoved him into Granddad's armchair. "Mom's not here," she said quickly, "and you have to listen. We can't leave the Lucky Star right now."

"Why not?" Mark's face was scrunched with frustration.

"Because Granddad's had a heart attack and Gran's getting over an operation for cancer," Sophie rushed on. "And Mom's quit her job in Vancouver so we can stay here and help them."

Mark's face went blank. "She quit her nursing job? You mean we're stuck here?" he whispered.

"For awhile." Sophie gulped. She knew how badly Liv wanted to stay permanently. She and Mom did, too. "You'll get used to the ranch," she promised. "I know how you feel. When I first came I hated it."

"You don't know how I feel!" Mark sprang to his feet. "I didn't even want to come but I had nowhere else to go. Dad and Elise kicked me out. They said I was hanging with a bad crowd and doing drugs." He glared at Sophie. "Drugs! I know I'm stupid, but I'm not brain dead."

"You're not stupid," Sophie cried angrily. "How dare they say that about you?"

"Forget it!" Mark lurched across the floor to the stairs. "I don't want to talk about it anymore."

Shaking her head, Sophie watched him start for his room upstairs.

✳ ✳ ✳ ✳ ✳

On a cool evening ride to Wild Horse Creek canyon later that day, Sophie described her conversation with Mark. "He's not even like the same person," she finished. "Dad and his girlfriend have totally wrecked his self-esteem. And Mark hates the desert." She switched her reins to her other hand and gave a deep sigh. Cisco seemed to understand and sighed a big horse sigh too.

"No wonder." Liv turned to her. "He's only seen it from the highway and the Lucky Star ranch yard. He can't even imagine what it's really like!"

They rode in silence down the sandy trail to the canyon. Liv forgot her worries about Mark as they entered its cool depths. The clop of hoofs echoed off walls of red rock glowing in the setting sun. Birds sang their evening songs and the wind blew softly through the trees along the canyon floor.

Liv turned Cactus Jack toward the spring where the Lucky Star Horses grazed. Diego was there, and his son Bando, a colt born that spring. They were both beautiful steel-blue roans.

She dismounted and approached Bando with a horse treat in her hand. The colt frisked over and gently nibbled it from her. Then he stuck his head in her pocket, searching for more treats. She stroked his silky nose. "I wonder if *you've* seen my mystery stallion."

"Are you still thinking about that crazy horse?" Sophie rode up beside her.

"I think about him all the time, especially when I'm in this canyon." Liv looked up at the darkening cliffs. She had hoped for a glimpse of the powerful black horse with the white blaze and four white stockings. His spirit seemed to haunt the spring where she'd first seen him.

"You're obsessed." Sophie shook her head.

"Mark will never see the stallion, or any of this, if he doesn't ride." Liv waved her hand at the spring and the horses. "And without riding I'm scared he'll be terminally bored on the ranch! What if he freaks out and makes Mom drag us all back to Vancouver? Granddad and Gran couldn't live here on their own. They'd have to come back with us. It would mean the end of the Lucky Star."

"Do you think Mom would do that?"

"Maybe." Liv nodded grimly. "I know she's really worried about Mark."

❋ ❋ ❋ ❋ ❋

For the next week and a half, Sophie and Liv watched their brother withdraw more and more. Everything they tried to do to help him get used to life on the ranch backfired. When he helped feed the horses, he put the pitchfork through his tennis shoe and stabbed his big toe. "Danged useless city shoes," Granddad grumbled as

Sophie bandaged Mark's foot. "Might as well put slippers on a horse as those fool things on a man. Have to get you a pair of boots."

Mark wouldn't wear cowboy boots. He wouldn't wear jeans, either, or a wide-brimmed cowboy hat. He didn't go outside unless it was to go somewhere in the truck. The girls rode every day while he stayed in the house to call and text his Vancouver friends.

Things came to a head when Mom discovered how expensive it was and cut him off. After that he spent all his time playing games on his phone.

"I heard him on that thing after midnight," Gran said to Sophie in the kitchen one morning. "I don't think the boy sleeps much."

"Is that so!" Granddad looked up from the sink where he was filling a jug of water. "I'll put a stop to that!" He marched into the dining room, grabbed the phone out of Mark's hand, dropped it in the jug, marched outside and pitched the whole thing in the horses' water trough.

Mark was right behind him, livid with rage. "Dad's right," he shouted, as he plunged his arm into the trough's scummy water. "You're a bully!"

"That's your problem right there." Granddad shook his head. "You listen to that father of yours. He should never have let you waste your time with that – that video game nonsense!" He swung on his heel and stalked back toward the house.

"Stubborn! Bossy! Mean!" Mark flung the words after his grandfather.

Sophie and Liv dashed up to him. "He's not really mean," Sophie gasped. "He just wants you to like it here."

"Well, he's got a stupid way of showing it." Mark tried to shake the water out of his phone. "This better not be wrecked!"

Liv reached into the trough for the water jug. "If you'd only get out more …" she started to say.

"Get OUT?" Mark gave a harsh laugh and gestured around the bare ranch yard. "Why? To see all this wonderful scenery, and watch you two play with your horses? It's hotter than a grease fire, full of dust and the dumb-ugliest place I've ever been in my life. There's nothing to get out for – nothing!"

He turned and headed back for the house scuffing the toes of his tennis shoes, sending up his own dust cloud as if he could hide in it.

"It *is* hot and dusty," Sophie admitted, staring after Mark. "And if we didn't have Cactus Jack and Cisco to ride, we might think it was boring too."

"Never!" Liv protested, but Sophie had a point. What would she do with herself if she wasn't practicing with her drill team or riding Cactus Jack across the desert at dawn and dusk when it was cool enough to ride? What would she do if she didn't have a dream about the Lucky Star Ranch? She had been checking the Rescue Station every night for news of her mystery stallion but there had been nothing since that first, blurry picture.

"Let's go groom the horses in the barn," she suggested. "Maybe we can think of something for Mark to do."

It was cooler in the barn. Sophie swooped her brush along Cisco's smooth side. He leaned into the brushing, enjoying it. She rested her forehead against his shoulder. "We need a secret weapon to make Mark like it here."

There was a low laugh from the open barn doorway. "Hey, where is everybody? I came to meet this mysterious brother of yours."

CHAPTER 5
Secret Weapon, Secret Plan

Liv looked up in surprise. "Dayna! What are you doing here?" Dayna Regis, as usual, looked amazing. She was wearing a powder blue leather jacket with a wide fringe, fitted jeans and blue cowboy boots. Her blonde hair was pulled pack in a sleek ponytail under a western hat. Dayna lived on the next ranch, the Silver Spur, where her parents ran a spa and raised palomino horses.

"I came to show off my new filly, and to meet your brother Mark." Dayna took off her large sunglasses in the dim barn. "I heard he'd come over a week ago. Where have you been hiding him?"

Liv shot a glance at Sophie. Mark was going to hate Dayna. He'd think she was shallow and showy. That's how she and Sophie had reacted when they first met her, but they had come to realize there was more to the seventeen-year-old than her rodeo star appearance. Dayna was a top-rated barrel racer, and inside that glossy shell she was hiding a broken heart.

Weeks ago the boy she loved, Temo Escobar, had gone to Mexico with his family. Since then, there'd been dark circles under Dayna's eyes.

"Mark's in the house." Sophie put her brush back in the grooming box. "He's kind of shy."

"You know me and shy guys!" Dayna grinned. "I can *usually* persuade them to come out of their shells." She turned with a swish of fringe and headed out the barn door. Her two-horse trailer stood in the yard with a young palomino tied to its side.

"Don't you think Mark will lo-ove this little girl?" Dayna straightened her long golden mane. "She's so pretty – going to be a champion, once I train her."

"Honestly, Dayna," Liv had dashed after her. "Mark's not into horses."

"Is that him?" Dayna asked. Mark was walking across the ranch yard, head bare, blinking in the bright sunlight. His eyes were fixed on Dayna's shiny red truck, parked in the ranch yard. Like everything belonging to the Silver Spur ranch, it was the hottest pickup truck on the market.

"Whose truck?" he started to say, and then stopped dead at the sight of Dayna.

"Howdy." She strode forward, fringe swinging. "It's my truck. Do you like it? You must be Mark."

"Yes, I … uh … sure," Mark stammered. "It's a beauty."

"This is Dayna Regis." Liv hurried up to them. "She's our neighbor." She wished Mark wouldn't stare at Dayna like that. She was worried he was going to say something really rude!

Instead he sputtered, "Your family has a spa?" He pointed to the sign on the side of the truck.

"That's right." Dayna tipped her head to one side. "We're neighbors – the next ranch over. And this here," she indicated the filly, "is my new horse, Gilded Lily. Isn't she sweet?"

She turned to Liv. "That reminds me! I had another reason for comin' over." She fished in her vest pocket and pulled out an envelope. "Here's two tickets to the natural horsemanship clinic at Fort Parson on Saturday. I'm taking Champagne. Bring Cactus Jack and Cisco. You'll love it.'

She put her sunglasses back on. "Is Shane around? I wanted him to help drive the four-horse trailer to Fort Parson, if he can spare the time." She smiled at Mark. "You come too! We can always use another strong arm with that big rig of ours."

"Well, I…uh…" Mark turned pink around the ears.

"Oh, come on. There's plenty of room in the truck."

Mark was glancing back and forth from the truck to Dayna. "Maybe," he finally gasped. "Maybe I'll come."

"Sure you will," Dayna said. "Come on, girls, help me get Gilded Lily out of the sun and I'll tell you all about this clinic. See you Saturday, Mark."

"I think you might be our secret weapon, Dayna." Sophie grinned as they led the filly into the shade of the barn.

"I don't know what you're talking about, but your brother's kind of cute."

Liv had been studying the ticket envelope. "We'll explain later, but what are these tickets all about? I didn't know you were interested in natural horsemanship. And why pay for places for Sophie and me before you found out if *we* were interested?"

Liv picked up her soft brush and went back to work on Cactus Jack's coat. He blew softly into her shoulder as if to say he was glad she hadn't forgotten him there in the cross ties.

"The trip's not about the clinic." Dayna took a deep breath and threw back her shoulders. "That's just an excuse to get the use of the horse trailer." She stepped closer, turned to see if anyone was listening, then whispered, "Don't tell anybody – not even your brother, but I've been in touch with Temo. He wants me to bring his horse Helado down to the border. I need Shane because I can't handle that ornery paint on my own. Ever since Temo left he's been a wild thing. My dad's been threatening to have him shot!"

Liv gasped, "Wow! What would your dad say if he knew you were going to see Temo?"

"He won't know. That's why I signed up for the horse clinic. Fort Parson is just a couple of miles north of the border. Temo has an aunt living there."

Fort Parson! Liv thought with a jolt. *I think that's near the rescue station where my mystery stallion might be!*

Just then they heard footsteps and a thud. Someone had come into the barn and tripped over a water bucket. "Shane?" Sophie called.

"No it's me, Brady." A brown-haired boy, taller than Mark with legs too long for his body, held out the empty bucket. "Sorry. I'll get you some more water. Hey, girls …" His shy grin was all for Liv. "Was that your brother I saw out there inspecting Dayna's truck like he wanted to eat it?"

"That's Mark," Liv laughed. "Trucks are one of his weaknesses."

"He needs a hat or he's gonna scorch that bald white head of his," Brady warned.

Liv sighed, "We're working on it."

"Leave it to me," said Dayna. "We'll tell him he can't come to Fort Parson unless he's wearin' the right clothes."

"Fort Parson?" Brady said eagerly.

"Yeah. We're all going to a horse clinic down there on Saturday. They've got a workshop on natural hoof trimming if you're interested." Dayna winked at Liv. "Plenty of room in the truck."

"Sure, that'd be great!" Brady's grin spread to his whole face. He glanced at his watch. "Well, see you, then. I should get going. Just stopped by to meet Mark. I'll say hello on my way out."

"Thanks for inviting Brady," Liv said later when Brady had gone. "I haven't had much chance to see him this summer. I'm not even sure how he feels about me."

"Don't thank me." Dayna shrugged. "The more people come along, the less suspicious my dad's going to be. And Brady can help with Helado. It might take more than Shane to get that horse in the trailer."

CHAPTER 6
Ready To Roll

"His name means 'ice cream' in Spanish," Dayna said. "But there's nothing cool about Helado." Dayna, Liv, Sophie, Brady and Mark were standing outside a fence in the shade of a live oak tree, watching the black and white horse careen around the corral at Dayna's ranch. Jess had dropped them at the Silver Spur first thing in the morning so they could help with Helado.

Only the paint horse was in motion. Everything else in the Arizona desert this hot Saturday morning sought the shade. The other horses crowded together beneath the trees on the far side of the corral. The rattlesnakes hid under rocks, the desert rats were deep in their holes. Long-eared foxes lounged in the shelter of the mesquite bushes beyond the barns.

"You need a hat." Dayna squinted up at Mark's shaved head. "Five minutes in that sun and your head's gonna glow like a red lightbulb."

"Don't worry about me," Mark mumbled. "We'll be going soon, won't we?"

"Soon as Shane gets here." Dayna glanced at her watch and whispered in Sophie's ear, "I want to be out of here before my father gets back from town and sees that I'm taking Temo's horse." The long white horse trailer was parked behind them, packed with everything they needed for the trip to Fort Parson – lots of water, extra gas, hay and horse treats.

"Won't he notice he's gone?" Liv twisted her thick brown hair into a knot and stuffed it under her hat to keep it off her neck.

"I'll make up some story." Dayna shrugged. "Dad won't care as long as he doesn't see us loading Helado. Once he's on board we'll load Champagne, pick up your horses and be ready to roll."

"I can't wait." Liv hugged herself. She had a secret plan. On the internet map it looked as though the Gila Flats rescue station was somewhere just north of Fort Parson. They might be able to take a side trip to look at the black stallion she'd seen in the picture.

At the same time, Liv kept her eye on Brady. He was his usual cheerful, goofy self, tripping on water buckets, bumping into her. But did it mean anything? Since their adventure in the Heartbreak Hotel he hadn't said a word that would indicate he thought of her as anything more than a friend.

Sophie kept glancing back at the dirt road to see if there was a plume of dust from Shane's pickup in the distance. Even though she knew Shane didn't want to be more than a good friend, time seemed to stop when he wasn't around and start again when he came near.

The patch of shade under the oak tree shrank as the sun rose higher. "Here, bro." Liv whipped off the bandanna she wore around her neck. She tied the corners into a makeshift hat, and tossed it to Mark. "Wear this. It's better than nothing."

"I'll look stupid." Mark flung it back.

"Not as stupid as you'll look with your head blistered and peeling," Liv pointed out.

"You're not in the rainforest now." Dayna turned and marched to the trailer, opened the front door and took a straw wide-brimmed hat off a hook. "Put this thing on your head, Mark Winchester. Do it for me."

Mark blushed red. He tried the hat, made a face and whipped it off. "Vancouver isn't the rainforest, and this dumb hat feels weird."

"That's 'cause you have no hair," Brady pointed out with a grin. "When it grows in a bit it will fit you better."

"Why is my hair any of your business?" Mark snarled.

"He was just trying to help!" Liv felt a spurt of anger at her brother.

"Can't you all just *leave me alone!*" Mark moved away to stand in what was left of the shade.

"You're as stubborn as a mule," Dayna shot after him. "I guess you get that from your grandfather, Ted Starr."

Sophie saw Mark wince. Being compared with Granddad was the worst thing he could imagine!

"Here comes Shane, so we can quit arguing and get going," Brady announced as an ancient pickup rattled up the Silver Spur drive. Sophie saw him give Mark a puzzled glance, wondering what was wrong with her brother. Everybody knew it was crazy to be out in the sun without a decent hat.

Shane parked near the corral and jumped out. "Sorry I'm late," he apologized with a shake of his head. "I got kinda – tied up at home – and then I had to leave Tux locked in the trailer, which he hates." The others nodded. No one asked for details. They all knew Shane lived with his dad in a small travel trailer on the road to Rattlesnake Bend. They knew his dad was a problem.

Whatever had happened at home that morning didn't stop Shane taking charge.

"Helado," he soothed in a low voice, walking purposefully toward the big paint horse. "You're going to see Temo, your best buddy."

Helado stood quietly while Shane threw a lead rope over his neck and swiftly buckled the halter in place. The horse walked calmly through the gate of the corral and stepped into the trailer like it was the easiest thing in the world.

"How did you do that?" Dayna tipped her head to one side. "I couldn't get near the son of a gun the whole time he's been here."

Who is she kidding? Sophie thought. *Helado wasn't any trouble. There must be another reason Dayna wants Shane on this trip.* Jealousy flared for a second but Sophie shook it off as she banged the bar on Helado's trailer stall shut. Dayna wasn't interested in Shane – she was sure of that.

Meanwhile, Shane rubbed Helado's black and white forehead with a gloved hand. "He's a pretty smart horse," he said. "I think he understands where he's goin'."

Dayna led her palomino, Champagne, in next. As a show horse, the mare had been trailered many times. She behaved like a pampered lady on her way to a spa.

"Nothin' to it." Dayna grinned at Mark as she hopped into the driver's seat. "Let's go get the rest of our load. Mark, climb in beside me."

The scowl faded from Mark's face as he slid in beside Dayna. Sophie took the window seat in front.

"Where do you want to sit?" Brady asked Liv shyly.

"Beside you?" Liv straightened her hat. "I'll sit between you and Shane so you can stretch out your long legs."

Brady just nodded. *This is so-o frustrating!* Liv thought. *He could say something.*

"We'll switch positions when we stop," Dayna promised. "I want Shane to do some of the driving."

It was a fast trip to the Lucky Star, where Liv and Sophie had already prepared Cactus Jack and Cisco for the trip. Dayna left the engine running while they loaded them. "It's gonna be a real hot day," she said, glancing up at the sky. "We'll need to leave the air on in the trailer the whole way."

Luckily, Cactus Jack and Cisco were seasoned travelers and easy loaders. Liv made sure they were comfortable, then closed the big side ramp with Brady's help. She couldn't stop a shiver of pleasure at the thought that they'd spend the whole day together – most of it side by side in the back seat of the truck.

Jess came out to see them off. "This is quite a load," she said, peering into the back of the trailer. "What time will you be back?"

Dayna consulted her watch. "Two hours there, two back, plus four hours at the clinic. With any luck we'll be home before dark." Liv saw a shadow cross Dayna's usually sunny face. Her visit with Temo wouldn't be nearly long enough for her!

"I hope you kids and your horses have a really good time at the clinic." Jess looked hopefully at Mark.

"Mom seems so relieved to be getting Mark out of the house," Sophie whispered to Liv as they climbed into the double cab of Dayna's truck.

"I know." Liv nodded. "I think she's afraid Granddad will have another heart attack if he has to look at Mark flopped on the couch much longer."

Dayna straightened herself behind the wheel, checked her side mirrors and put the big red truck in gear.

"Okay, *amigos*," she sang out to her five passengers. "We've got a straight run on a paved road all the way to Fort Parson. No problem!"

A straight run on a paved road, Liv sighed to herself, looking at a road map spread out on her lap. *It looks like the Gila Flats Rescue Station isn't far off this road. If I could just get there, I could see, once and for all, if they have our mystery stallion.*

On the seat in front of Liv Sophie shuddered as if someone had slipped an ice cube down the back of her tee shirt. *No problems?* She wished Dayna hadn't said that! Sophie's experience with the Arizona desert had taught her that problems were everywhere! Poisonous snakes, cougars, stampedes, floods, dangerous smugglers driving ATVs. They were all out there between them and Fort Parson.

CHAPTER 7
The Road to Gila Flats

Maybe I was wrong, Sophie thought as the red truck and big white trailer zoomed down the highway an hour later. *Maybe this will be one trip where nothing goes wrong. If we can just think of a way to keep Mark busy while we ...*

"Ohhhh! There's the road!" Liv's sudden shriek shook the truck. "Dayna, stop – please!"

The truck swerved dangerously toward the shoulder of the road. "What's wrong?" Dayna shouted, checking her side mirror to make sure the trailer hadn't jack-knifed.

Liv jabbed at the map on her lap. "The Gila Flats Rescue Station. We just drove right past the turn off."

"What turn off? What are you talking about? Shane, calm that crazy girl down!" Dayna sounded like her father Sam Regis at that moment.

"Take it easy." Shane tipped back his hat. "What are you trying to tell us, Liv?"

"The rescue station, Gila Flats. It was back there, down a dirt road." Liv stabbed at the map to show him. "Please turn around, Dayna, and go back."

Dayna pumped the brakes and the truck slowed to a stop. "This better be important," she muttered. "It's not good for the horses to stop and start."

Liv looked frantically from Shane to Brady. "It's our mystery stallion," she gasped. "I think they have him at Gila Flats. I didn't realize till I looked at the map that there's a road right to it from here."

"What is she talking about?" Mark leaned over to ask Sophie.

"It's a horse." Sophie stared in amazement at Liv. Why hadn't she shared this information? "There's a big black stallion that we've seen a couple of times since we got here."

"Oh, a horse. Of course that would be a good reason to nearly drive off the road." Mark rolled his eyes. "But why would he be at a rescue station?"

"Because he's wild. He attacked Granddad's stallion, Diego, and ran off with his mares." Sophie started to explain.

"Our mares, too," Dayna joined in. "Dad hired a helicopter to hunt him down."

"But a lightning storm saved him," Liv explained in a

rush, "and he got away just as they were going to shoot him." She turned to Shane. "You saw him run, Shane. I'll never get that picture of him streaking across the valley out of my mind, will you? You'd like to see him again, wouldn't you?"

"Well, yeah," Shane admitted. "But we can't go tearing off in the desert with this load, and you don't know for sure if it's our mystery horse at the rescue station."

"No, but..." Liv gulped. "What if it is?"

"Let me see the map." Dayna reached into the back seat to grab it. She ran her finger down the highway and then pointed to Gila Flats. "Look. It's on a small track. There's no telling what condition the road's in, or how long it would take us to get there."

Brady said eagerly, "He saved us from the horse smugglers by kicking down that ghost town hotel."

"But what good is it going to be to see him?" Sophie argued. "What could we do?"

Liv shouted, "What could we do? We have a ranch, we have a horse trailer behind this truck!"

Dayna bit her lip and glanced at the dashboard clock. "Forget it. We can't pick up another horse. The trailer's fully loaded now. Anyway, I promised Temo I'd be there in an hour. We're already late."

"Maybe we can stop there on the way back?" Liv begged. "After we drop off Helado?"

Dayna shook her blonde head firmly. "I'm not risking

the trailer on a rough road. And if it was the same black stallion, and we took him home, your Granddad or my father would just shoot him. You'd better forget the whole thing." She started the truck.

"We can come down another time." Brady put a comforting hand on her arm. "We know where Gila Flats is now. You and I and Shane and Sophie and Mark."

"Leave me out of it," grunted Mark.

"But we're *here now*. Look, there's the road!" Liv ground her teeth in helpless fury. She twisted in her seat and peered out the back window at the sign for Gila Flats. It was just a white plank on a stake, pointing down a road across the desert, but it felt like destiny calling. How could they speed right past like this? It was wrong!

In the front seat, Sophie let out her breath in a sigh of relief. She was used to Liv's sudden crazy ideas, and also used to Liv getting her way. Her twin sister was so forceful and always sure she was right. Like about this stallion. Sophie knew with every fiber of her being that it would be a mistake to go chasing down that road after the mystery stallion. At the same time, she could feel Liv's frustration coming at her in waves. As if somehow, this was all her fault!

✳ ✳ ✳ ✳ ✳

At Fort Parson, Liv and Sophie discovered the real reason Dayna had brought Shane along. They parked on a wide street with small stucco houses. One of them belonged to

Temo's aunt, Nina. Dayna left the engine running while she dashed inside and came out arm-in arm with Temo.

"*Buenos dias, compadres*!" As the others climbed out of the truck to greet him, the smile on Temo's face stretched from ear to ear. He had closely-cropped black hair and laughing brown eyes. "So you brought me my horse … and my girl. *Muchas gracias*."

Shane opened the side door of the big trailer and Temo hopped in. "*Hola*, Helado, *muy bueno*!" He spoke softly in Spanish to his horse, then led him down the ramp. "*Gracias amigos*," Temo thanked them again, stroking his horse's cheek. "It's so good to have him back – and to see all of you."

"This is our brother Mark," Liv introduced him to Temo.

"Pleased to meet you." Temo nodded politely.

Mark squinted at the good-looking Temo as if he suddenly felt like four flat tires. Liv knew the feeling. She'd had a crush on Temo, but when you saw him with Dayna you knew you had no chance.

Dayna's eyes shone with happiness. "Shane, can you drive Mark, Brady and the girls over to the fairgrounds for the clinic? I'll meet you there at four."

"Sure." Shane grinned. "My pleasure."

"Thanks, everybody." Dayna waved as they piled into the truck with Shane at the wheel. "Enjoy the clinic."

"I guess this is what she meant by having *you* take a

shift at driving," teased Sophie, sitting beside him. "Just a way to get rid of the rest of us!"

"I guess so," Shane agreed. "Seems like she had it all worked out. Even programmed the directions to the fairgrounds on the truck's GPS so I wouldn't get lost." He pointed to the instrument panel. "Looks like I make a turn at the stop sign."

CHAPTER 8
Discovery!

The large indoor exhibition center at the Fort Parson fairgrounds provided a huge parking lot for trailers. Shane parked skillfully, turned off the ignition and smiled at Sophie. "Let's get these horses unloaded," he said. "What are you going to do with Champagne? We can't leave her in the trailer with the air-conditioning off."

"I'm sure there'll be a stall for her inside." Sophie smiled back. "What I mean is, Dayna registered for the clinic." Why did Shane's grin give her butterflies inside? It was hard to be "just friends" when he looked at her like that!

Inside was a scene of organized confusion, with people and horses milling around the stabling area. Sophie and Liv found the stalls assigned for their three horses side-by-side.

Liv straightened Champagne's golden mane as she settled her in her stall. "You'll be fine in here, girl. Lots of hay, water, clean shavings; everything a horse could desire and you don't even have to work."

She closed the stall door and reached for Cactus Jack's lead rope from Brady. "As for you," she told her horse, "you'd better make me proud today." She glanced at Mark, who had been looking glum since Dayna left. "What are you guys going to do – watch us ride?"

"I think we'll wander around." Brady grinned. "This looks like a girl thing."

"Just because the instructor is a woman and most of the riders are female doesn't mean it's for girls!" Liv protested.

"There's other stuff happening." Shane consulted a program. "A horse whisperer working with mustangs and a workshop on natural hoof trimming."

"Whoop-de-doo," Mark muttered under his breath. "Hoof trimming."

"Come on, you'll like the mustangs." Brady led him off. "Lots of excitement."

Liv and Sophie watched them go. "Shane and Brady are really trying to help," Sophie said. Mark walked between the two cowboys, his floppy tennis shoes, baggy, low-slung pants and black hoodie a sharp contrast to their high-heeled cowboy boots, trim jeans, plaid shirts, vests and western hats.

Liv nodded. "I wish Mark would be nicer to them. He's sarcastic to Shane and acts like Brady doesn't exist."

"Mark's being a jerk," Sophie agreed. "But he must feel like he'll never belong. Look at him, Liv. This isn't going to work."

✳ ✳ ✳ ✳ ✳

"The horse whispering is in there." Shane showed Mark the large arena with its stadium seats. "The hoof-trimming is outside."

Mark looked at the dim, empty space. "I'll sit up there." He pointed to the deserted stands.

"It should start soon," Brady told him. "You know where we are, and where the girls are. You'll be all right?"

"Don't worry about me." Mark took off, loping up the stands.

"He won't get beat up by somebody if we leave him, will he?" Brady stared after him. "He looks so weird."

"Not here." Shane pushed back his hat. "But I wouldn't want to leave Mark alone on the main street of Fort Parson at night."

"What's the matter with him?" Brady asked.

Shane shook his head. "Family stuff – with his dad. Can be rough."

"Yeah, I guess." Brady shut up. Shane had his own troubles with *his* father so he understood Mark. Brady suddenly felt lucky. His own dad was a great guy – always there when you needed him.

✳ ✳ ✳ ✳ ✳

Mark played his video games until the lights in the arena

came on. People trickled in. A crew with a tractor brought in sections of tall fencing and created a round pen inside the arena space, right below where he was sitting.

He tried to scrunch into the shadows, become invisible, disappear into his video game. He hated the way everybody stared at him here, as if he was some kind of freak.

A guy with a headset mike had walked quietly into the arena. He opened the gate of the round pen and went in. The mike crackled. "My name is Buck Barnes," the man announced. "In a minute I'm going to be joined in this pen by a wild horse. I'm going to ask this horse to trust me enough to let me get a halter on. If I'm lucky, a bridle and saddle. I'm going to demonstrate how you can begin to train a wild horse using no force, only persuasion."

"Big phony," Mark groaned to himself. This sounded like a circus performance! No wonder Brady and Shane weren't interested. He got up to leave, but as he wove his way down the stands, a gate opened at the end of the arena and two cowboys half led, half dragged in a small paint horse, quivering with fear.

Mark stopped. He sat down, closer to the bottom of the arena, fascinated despite himself. The cowboys led the mustang through the gate of the round pen, slipped off the ropes around his neck and went out, clanging the gate behind them.

The mustang took off at a run around the pen, desperate

57

for a way out. It kept as far away from the man in the center as it could.

Buck turned with the horse. "He's frightened by the loud noise, and the strangeness of everything here," he said softly into the mike. "You notice I don't look directly at his head, but keep my attention at his shoulder."

After a while the small paint horse tired and stopped galloping. It stood, pressed against the tall round fence with his hind end facing the trainer. Buck pointed his whip at the paint's haunches and snapped it in the air. The paint took off again like a shot, and again Buck followed him with his body. He kept the whip low, but when the horse turned a disrespectful hip to him or twirled his head, the trainer raised it and made him run again.

Before long the paint horse stopped and faced the man. "That's what I've been waiting for," Buck told the crowd in the same soft, low voice. "See how he's licking his lips and – oh, good, a yawn. That means he might be ready to join up. Let's see."

Buck turned his back on the mustang and took a few steps. The mustang followed. Buck took a few more steps and the horse did too. Finally it was following him around the pen, and when Buck turned the horse didn't spook but stood and let Buck stroke his neck and withers.

Fake! Mark told himself as the trainer put a halter on the mustang. *That horse was never really afraid. He's not really wild. The whole thing's just an act!*

He sat through a couple more horses just to make sure he was right. That was enough – he was leaving. He was on his way out of the arena when a pounding crashing ruckus made him pause. In the dim light of the chute three men were struggling to control a black horse. It took all their strength and half a dozen ropes to get him to the round pen, and when they let him go he exploded. Buck Barnes spun in the center as the horse circled him at a furious gallop.

"I'm working with a real tough horse here," Buck almost croaked into the mike. "I can't promise anything with this wild stallion but I'm gonna try because this fellow deserves a chance. He's had some rough treatment at human hands, been hunted and chased and ended up at the Gila Flats Rescue Station."

Mark stopped as if he'd been flash frozen. A black horse, a stallion, from the Gila Flats Rescue Station? Wasn't that the place Liv wanted to stop? Wasn't her mystery horse black? Maybe he was wrong, but he knew how upset Liv would be if it was her horse and she missed him.

"I'd better find her," Mark said out loud, stumbling toward the exit. He could hear comments as he passed:

"That's one *loco* horse."

"Barnes is crazy to be in a small pen with that killer."

"He's gonna get himself hurt, you wait and see!"

Mark found Liv and Sophie watching the clinic leader and another rider when he stumbled into the smaller arena.

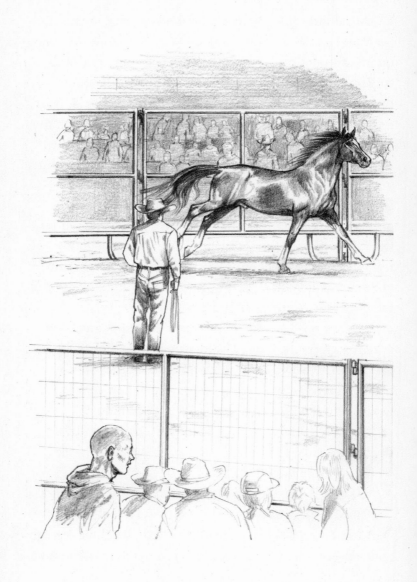

"Can I talk to you?" he hissed to Liv.

"Not now." Liv put her fingers to her lips.

"It's important."

Liv shot Sophie a look and they both squirmed from their seats past a row of annoyed onlookers.

"What is it, Mark?"

"That horse. The black horse you wanted to see – I think he might be here!"

"How could he be?" Sophie stared at her brother.

"Are you making this up?" asked Liv.

"No!" The words burst from Mark in frustration. "The horse trainer said he was wild but deserved a chance. He said something about the Gila Flats Rescue Station."

Liv didn't wait to hear more. "WHERE IS HE?"

"This way." Mark pushed his way through the crowd. "The horse trainer, Buck Barnes, is trying to work with him..." Mark turned for a second to scan Liv's face. "The horse looks like a monster, sis. Are you sure?"

"Of course. Hurry!" Liv shoved him forward into the arena. They raced along the boards till they were opposite the round pen at eye level.

"That's him!" Liv gasped to Sophie who was right behind her. "Look! The white blaze, the four white feet, the long, flowing mane and tail – that's Mystery!"

At last, Liv had given the black horse his name.

CHAPTER 9
Mystery Solved!

"He's perfect," Liv breathed in awe. "Look at the way he carries his head – so proud!"

"See that inside ear turned toward me?" Buck's soothing voice purred. "If we can get this stallion to join up, he has loads of potential."

"I never thought I'd see him *this* calm," Sophie marveled.

"Buck said he deserved a chance. What did he mean?" Mark yanked Liv's sleeve.

Liv glanced at her brother. His cheeks were flushed and his were eyes riveted to the action in the round pen.

"He means," she said brutally, "that Mystery is going to be culled, put down, destroyed, killed – unless someone can tame him. This is probably his last chance." *Is it possible Mark is starting to feel something about a horse?* she wondered.

"Give in, or die," Mark muttered. Every time the stallion turned in, head high, Buck sent him spinning around the ring again.

As they watched the stallion finally halted, sides heaving, froth dripping from the sides of his mouth. He lowered his head and turned toward Buck. His lower lip drooped.

Sophie reached out to squeeze Liv's hand. "He's going to join up."

Soon Buck had a loop of rope over Mystery's neck and was stroking his side. "I'm going to lead this big fellow back to his stall," he spoke softly into his mike. "He's had enough for today. And this will be our last horse this afternoon. I hope you enjoyed this demonstration of natural horse training."

People stood to applaud Buck Barnes and the beautiful black horse.

Their applause came too soon.

As Buck led Mystery toward the end of the arena they passed close enough to Liv, Mark and Sophie to almost touch the horse's sweaty body, feel the hot breath from his nostrils.

All at once, Mystery stopped dead. His head flew up. His ears flattened against his skull. His nostrils flared and Liv could see the whites of his eyes.

"What's wrong with him?" Mark exclaimed.

Liv glanced to her left where Mystery's eyes were

fixed, glaring. Two stocky men wearing ball caps were leaning over the rail. Liv clutched Sophie's arm. "Look! It's the coyotes – the horse smugglers – who captured Mystery! I'd know them anywhere."

So did Mystery. He ripped the rope out of Buck's hand, reared high in the air and lunged at the two men. They flew backwards and scrambled away as his hoofs flailed at the arena boards.

Mystery's scream of fury brought officials running. Ropes zinged through the air, hauling the powerful stallion to his knees.

"What happened?" Mark's voice rang with shock.

"Those men," Liv raced to explain, "wanted Mystery for stallion fights – for gamblers to bet on. They had him shut up in an old ghost town. Brady and I got him free and he was so mad at those guys he tried to kill them."

"I hope they didn't recognize us." Sophie shivered. "We wrecked their truck, remember?"

"Never mind that." Liv brushed aside the danger. "I'll bet you anything they still want him. I'll bet they came here on purpose to upset him. Now they'll offer to take him off the Rescue Station's hands. They'll ship him over the border to be a fighting stallion."

She paused, breathless. "I've got to get help, stop those coyotes." She took off, running.

"She's insane!" Mark stared after her.

"Totally," Sophie gasped. "But when did that ever stop

her?" She dragged Mark to the exit. "We've got to find Shane and Brady."

"Why do they call those guys coyotes?" Mark asked as they hurried through the crowded hall toward the hoof trimming workshop.

"Because they're sneaky and fast and it's hard to catch them smuggling people and other stuff across the Mexican border," Sophie told him.

She and Mark collected Shane and Brady and a few minutes later all four of them met a frantic Liv searching for them. "I was right!" she exclaimed. "The Rescue Station wrote Mystery off as a lost cause after he went crazy in the arena, and the coyotes claimed him."

"Those two lowlifes?" Shane looked grim. "They're dangerous." One of the men had hit him over the head with a branding iron at their last meeting.

"They didn't do it directly," Liv moaned. "Some smooth-talking guy was fronting for them. I heard the whole thing."

"Did they see you?" Sophie asked.

"Don't know, don't care. They'll take Mystery back to Gila Flats to get the paperwork done. We've got to go there – explain!"

"Hold it." Shane took Liv by the shoulders. "We have to wait for Dayna and then load three horses before we can go anywhere."

"We can call the Rescue Station," Brady suggested. "Give them a heads up."

"Where's your phone, Mark? It's worth a try." Liv squirmed out of Shane's grip. "Search their number."

Mark fished in the front pocket of his hoodie where he kept his phone, then in his deep pants' pockets. "It's not here!"

"You must have put it down while you were watching Buck Barnes work with Mystery," Sophie said. "Let's go back to the arena and look."

The arena was full of spectators for a reining demonstration. Liv searched the benches and the floor at people's feet, but Mark's phone was gone.

"I can't lose it!" Mark turned white. "My whole life is in that phone. All my contacts, everything!"

"Let's try the Lost and Found." Brady tried to calm him down.

"Meanwhile, Mystery is slipping further out of our reach," Liv groaned. "You and your stupid phone!"

The girl behind the lost and found counter shook her head when they asked about Mark's phone. He left her a slip of paper with the ranch's number in case someone turned it in.

"You can't rescue every horse you come across," Shane said quietly as they left the Lost and Found.

"Mystery's not just any horse!" Liv shot back. "We watched him go from crazy wild to tame in the pen with Buck Barnes."

Brady said matter-of-factly, "But he's still a wild stallion."

"Granddad wouldn't want him anywhere near the ranch." Sophie gave a firm shake of her head. "You know how furious he was when the stallion hurt Diego."

"*Granddad* shouldn't be the only one who decides," Mark muttered, suddenly emerging from a cloud of gloom about his phone. "Buck Barnes said the black horse had a lot of potential."

"Thank you, Mark!" Liv gasped with relief to have at least one person on her side. "So come on, let's go before they ship Mystery out of here."

"Wait a minute." Shane tipped back his hat. "Even if we could get our hands on the stallion, Dayna wouldn't agree to ..."

"I wouldn't agree to what?" Dayna asked. She had marched into the middle of the group, her chin up, her eyes red. "By the way, Temo said to say goodbye to all of you. He … he's going back to Mexico tomorrow." She swiped her eyes dry and listened with an intent frown as Liv described what had happened to Mystery.

"Stallion fighting is just plain disgusting," she said with a toss of her head. "And Temo hates the coyotes. He says they exploit and betray helpless people. Besides, the one time he saw that black stallion I know he was very impressed. He wouldn't want those thugs to have him." Her frown changed to a grin. "Let's stop them. We'll use the phone in the truck."

"Thanks, Dayna." Liv shot her a grateful smile as they threaded their way toward the exit.

They trooped out of the building into the stunning afternoon heat. The parking lot sizzled like a hot skillet. At its far edge they saw a small horse trailer hitched to a gray pickup. Heading toward it were the two coyotes, leading a stumbling black horse.

"Mystery!" Liv started to run, despite the heat. "What have you done to him?" she shouted.

The men, startled, looked back over their shoulder. "What business is it of yours?" one of them asked in a Spanish accent.

"Get away!" The other made a menacing gesture.

Liv looked desperately around for help.

"Come on." Shane caught up to her and grabbed her arm. "These guys are nothing to mess with. I've still got a dent in my head where they hit me with that branding iron."

"I know, but we can't let them take him." Liv twisted away from Shane's grip.

The men had opened the trailer door and were lowering the ramp. Mystery stood placidly, his head down.

The others rushed up to join Liv and Shane. "We're going to call the Rescue Station and tell them who you are!" Dayna threatened. "And I'm sure the border police will be interested."

The two coyotes waved her off as if she was an annoying insect.

"It's no use," Shane insisted. "We can't do anything

68

here." They headed off toward Dayna's rig, Brady pulling a reluctant Liv along. As they reached the red truck a tall man in a big hat strolled toward an SUV parked beside it.

"Hey! That's Buck Barnes, the horse whisperer guy." Liv dashed ahead. "Buck, Mr. Barnes," she called out, "can we speak to you for a minute?"

"You want my autograph?" Buck pulled a pen from his vest pocket.

"No sir, I mean, yes I'd *love* your autograph, but right now it's about the black horse you were training in there." She pointed toward the coyotes, still struggling to load Mystery.

A scowl creased Buck's handsome face. "Not one of my successes." He unlocked his car door and slid behind the wheel. "Sorry. I have to be going now."

Dayna grabbed the door. "Did you know that he's being taken by horse smugglers to be a fighting stallion?"

Buck took in Dayna's appearance, and read the name on her truck. "Are you Dayna Regis, from the Silver Spur ranch?"

"Yes, I am."

"I know your father." Buck got out of the driver's seat. "Are you and your friends in some kind of trouble? What's this about the stallion?"

"He's over there." Dayna pointed again. "Those two men have him drugged or they wouldn't be able to get him near their trailer. They were the ones who spooked him."

"It wasn't your fault," Liv added quickly. "The reason the stallion spooked is that they captured and tortured him in the past."

"Really?" Buck looked intrigued.

"You did a great job in the ring with him," Sophie added.

Buck shut his car door. "Thanks. What did you want me to do?"

"We'd like to take him … back to the Silver Spur," Dayna said, making this up as she went along. "But the Rescue Station has released him to those men. Can you do anything about that?"

"I'm not sure …" Buck stared around the ring of worried faces. His gaze fixed on Mark. "Hey! Weren't you the young fellow watching me earlier in the demonstration?"

Mark nodded. "Yeah, but how did you notice me? You had your eyes on the horses the whole time."

"It might look that way, son." Buck grinned. "But a good trainer has to be aware of everything around him, the same way a horse is." His grin faded. "Now that you bring it to mind, I remember those two fellows leaning over the boards just before the stallion went berserk. I believe you. Stay here, kids. I'll see what I can do."

CHAPTER 10
On the Road Again

Liv hopped anxiously on the hot pavement. "I hope Buck Barnes hurries; the coyotes have got Mystery loaded already."

"Here he comes." Sophie pointed to the exhibition hall doors. Buck emerged between two hulking security guards with guns at their sides.

The three strode to the coyotes' truck. After a short conversation with a lot of arm waving, Mystery was led out of the trailer. The two men slammed the trailer shut, jumped in their truck and rattled away with the security men watching.

Buck led Mystery across the hot pavement to Liv.

"Here's your stallion." He offered her Mystery's lead rope. "I'll help you load him. I straightened things out with the authorities."

Liv approached the stallion cautiously. "How is he?"

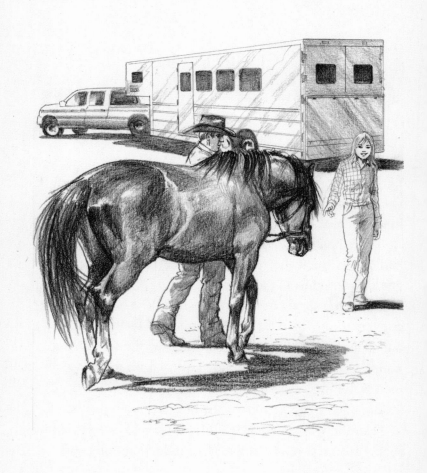

It was the closest she'd ever been to Mystery. Even drugged, he gave off a tremendous sense of bottled up power.

"He'll be fine." Buck grinned his large grin. "But it might be a good idea to get him back to your ranch before the sedative they gave him wears off."

"We'll go get our horses and load them as fast as we can." Liv and Sophie set off for the stables at top speed.

Shane and Brady swung open the big trailer doors. The heat inside was stifling.

"I'll start the truck," Dayna gasped to Shane. "We need to get the air conditioning going, fast!"

As the engine of the big red pickup roared to life, Dayna flicked the instrument panel. She glanced at Shane in alarm. "The phone's not working. Dad's new GPS isn't either. What have you done to my truck?"

"Nothing," Shane promised. "Maybe the electronic system got fried in this heat. But we've got cool air blasting from all of the vents."

"I'm glad that's working! We couldn't haul horses today without air."

Once the trailer was cool, Buck and Shane loaded Mystery in Helado's empty stall. He stood quietly, head down, until Champagne, Cisco and Cactus Jack rattled into the other stalls. Then his head went up and his eyes brightened.

"You're going to be fine, aren't you?" Liv dared to

stroke his rough neck. "Thanks, Mr. Barnes. We'll take good care of him."

"I'll be in touch," he told them as he folded his long frame into the front seat of his SUV. "Good luck, and go straight home."

They waved goodbye and then turned to the heavily loaded trailer. Liv checked that they had enough water for the return trip. "I'll ride back here and make sure the horses are okay," she volunteered

"All right." Dayna nodded briefly. "But the trip might be a bit bumpy."

Sophie stared at her. "Why? The highway to Fort Parson was totally smooth."

"I'm not taking the highway home." Dayna studied the map. "That's why I wanted the GPS – to plot an alternate route. But it looks like if we take a right turn out of town and go over the Ocotillo Hills, we can get to our ranch before dark."

"Why would you go that way?" Sophie felt the familiar shiver of fear. *Hadn't Dayna said taking a rough road with four horses in a trailer was too dangerous?*

"You think the coyotes might follow us?" Light dawned in Liv's brain.

"Maybe. They know where I live." Dayna pointed to the bright lettering on her Silver Spur truck. "They'll think we're too chicken to take this big rig off-road. But

I'd sooner deal with a few bumps than be chased by guys with a grudge against us."

"You're so right." Liv turned to her twin. "Come on, Sophie, it'll be fine. Ride in the trailer with me so we can keep an eye on Mystery and the other horses."

I hate it when Liv gets that look in her eye, Sophie thought as she wedged herself into a corner of the trailer. *She loves any kind of adventure, the riskier the better!*

Meanwhile, Brady and Mark hopped in the back seat of the cab, Shane slid in beside Dayna. She chuckled as she steered the rig out of the parking lot.

"What are you laughing at?" Shane glanced at her from under the brim of his hat.

"I was thinking how my dad would feel about me rescuing Mystery! A wild Spanish colonial stallion, riding with one of his prize palominos. You know what a snob he is about the Lucky Star horses. Thinks they're good for nothing."

Shane grinned. "What is he going to say?"

"I can guess." Dayna's shoulders rose and fell. "Dad doesn't see anything good in being different, whether it's horses or people."

Shane knew she was thinking about Temo.

"I'm sorry." Dayna turned off on the side road at the edge of town. "I know you have troubles with your own father. I just wish mine didn't have a mind as stiff as a chunk of mesquite."

She turned over her shoulder to ask Mark, "How about your father? I guess he's hard to get along with or you wouldn't be here, right?"

"I didn't used to think he was," Mark muttered. "I thought we were a perfect family, Sophie, me, Liv and Mom. Then one day, BOOM, he runs off with dumb Elise. I hate them both. If it wasn't for them I wouldn't be stuck here in this, this … wilderness."

"We like our wilderness, don't we?" Dayna punched Shane in the arm. "Keeps us tough. And right now we're heading into the heart of it."

The desert ahead was littered with large square boulders. As the truck wound slowly upwards it looked as if a giant child had smashed a house of blocks. The Ocotillo Hills rose out of that litter, large cone-shaped mounds high above the desert floor. "That's the range we have to cross," Dayna said. "Check the map, Brady. We don't want to make a wrong turn."

❊ ❊ ❊ ❊ ❊

Behind, in the trailer, Sophie and Liv braced themselves against the hay bales as they rocked from side to side. Liv got up to look out the small back window. "We're halfway up the hills and I don't see anything following us. Of course it's too hazy to see the road down below."

"I'll be glad when we're on the other side." Sophie came to stand beside her at the window. "The thought of

76

those coyotes chasing us gives me the creeps. Especially up here where we're all alone."

"I never thought Dayna would be so brave," Liv admitted, plunking back down in the corner. "Ever since that day in the cave when Temo rescued her, she's a different person."

"And her life got *a lot* harder," Sophie added. "Her parents would never agree to her dating Temo."

"That's the trouble with liking someone too much." Liv wriggled into the hay. "I think I'm going to give up my crush on Brady."

"Why?"

"Well I'm not sure he really likes me. And if he doesn't, I don't want to get hurt."

Sophie was quiet. She wished she could give up "liking" Shane so much. It would hurt a lot less. "Sometimes you can't help the way you feel," she said at last.

"But you can try." Liv smiled at the four gorgeous horses: sorrel, chestnut, palomino and black. "Look at them!" she sighed. "Horses are so much more satisfying. Can you believe we've actually got our mystery stallion in this trailer and we're taking him home?"

"But what are we going to do with him when we get there?" Sophie had been worrying about this since they loaded Mystery.

Liv looked up at the huge black horse. His large brown eyes gazed back at her. They gleamed with life and intelligence. The drug was wearing off. Now they would have to deal with his true wild nature. "I don't know!" Liv cried. "I just know I'm not going to let him die."

Just then the trailer jolted to one side and stopped on a slant. Liv opened the front door and looked out. "What's the matter?" she called.

CHAPTER 11
Sidetracked!

Liv jumped out of the trailer. A beautiful high desert
scene spread before her. To the south, the Sierra Madre
Mountains rose hazy in the distance, red and gold.

Dayna and Brady were standing by the truck, trying to
keep the map from blowing away. A strong wind blasted the
top of the hill, threatening to tear the hats from their heads,
making it hard to hold the map still enough to read it.

Brady pointed ahead. "The road forks," he shouted,
"We're trying to figure out which way to go."

Liv saw that the road had narrowed to a single dirt
track. Above them on both sides the hills rose steeply.
Instead of dry scrub and cactus plants, shrub oak and
manzanita bushes blanketed the hillsides. They'd climbed
to a different zone of the desert, a high chaparral. One
branch of the road angled down, the other upward.

"The fork in the road isn't marked on the map," Brady

yelled over the rushing wind. "One of these must be a side track."

"Let's take the one going down." Dayna grabbed for her hat as it threatened to sail away. "We must be at the top of the pass with this wind."

"You're the driver," Brady yelled back. "But you know you can't turn this big rig around if the road gets too narrow."

"Can't stay here with the truck engine running." Dayna turned to Liv. "How are the horses riding?"

"Mystery's waking up, but we're okay." Liv made a thumbs up sign. "Nice and cool."

Just then, Mark and Shane stepped out of the cab on the passenger side.

"Get back in," Dayna hollered. "We're leaving."

Shane clapped a hand to his hat as he walked around the cab to her side. "Don't know about that, Dayna. The engine died. Didn't you hear?"

"Can't hear anything with this wind," Dayna bellowed. "Don't worry, we'll start it again!" She jumped into the driver's side and they heard her try to start the truck. Nothing. In seconds she was standing beside them again. "What's the matter with it?"

Shane shook his head. "Could be a lot of things. You aren't out of gas?"

"Of course not!"

Shane got down and looked under the truck. "No fuel

line leakin'. It must be the electrical system. That might be why your GPS and phone don't work. Maybe a wire worked itself loose."

"Or maybe those coyotes had something to do with it," Dayna said furiously. "If they messed with my truck, I'll ..." She stopped, realizing the danger of their situation. "Hey! We've got to get the horses out." She headed for the trailer. "Without the engine running there's no air-conditioning."

Sophie had appeared at the trailer's front door. "The air doesn't seem to be working. What's wrong?" she called.

"What's *wrong*?" Mark suddenly shouted, surprising all of them with the force of his anger. "We're stuck up here – that's what's wrong! The truck won't run and you're taking the horses out of the trailer." His voice rose. "What are you going to do then – ride them back to the ranch?"

"Steady." That was Shane. "We'll decide what to do once we get them out. Yelling and screaming isn't going to get us anywhere."

"I wasn't screaming." Mark turned away, shoulders hunched against the wind.

It's hard to believe, Sophie thought, *that they're both the same age. Shane seems like a man and Mark acts like a frightened little boy. Shane's right. Panic doesn't help. But we're in real trouble without a truck!*

Liv was already unfastening the trailer door, reaching

for Cactus Jack's lead rope. "Come on, Jack, ride's over," she told the chestnut, trying to keep the fear out of her voice. "Just a nice walk on a windy hilltop on a lovely hot day."

She tied Jack to the side of the trailer while they unloaded Champagne and Cisco. Now it was Mystery's turn. He stamped and pawed as Liv cautiously unfastened the stall bar. "The sedative's wearing off," she said to Brady. "It might be hard to unload him."

"If he decides to take off down the hill, we can't stop him." Brady took a firm grip on Mystery's lead rope. "Remember in the Heartbreak Hotel stable? He ripped the rope right out of my hand."

"I know," Liv said grimly. "I know we can't stop him from running away. But the worst that can happen is that he'll be free again."

"Free until the next time he's captured, or someone takes a shot at him," Brady reminded her.

"You're right, he doesn't have much of a chance running free. That's why I want to get him back to the Lucky Star. We can keep him safe till we think of another solution. And at least he isn't in the hands of those coyotes!"

The drug the horse smugglers had used was powerful. Although Mystery snorted and tossed his head as they led him out the trailer door, he didn't rear or kick. In ten minutes they had all four horses out, manes and tails blowing in the hot wind. Cactus Jack raised his head, sniffed the wind and whinnied loudly as Liv saddled him.

"What's that, Jack? Do you know the way back to our ranch?" Dayna shouted over the wind. "Cause I sure don't. It's one of these roads – but which one? Maybe the right?"

"Before we head out," Shane told her, "we'd better take what we need from the truck and the trailer. The horses can carry water. That's the most important thing. Food next, if we have any."

"Do you really think we'll be out here that long?" Mark's screechy voice asked. "How far are we from your ranch, Dayna?"

"If I knew where we are it would be easier to say." Dayna folded the map and stuffed it in Champagne's saddlebag. "It looked like thirty miles or so on the map. Maybe we've gone twenty, or less. That means ten or fifteen more to go – *if* we find the right road. At least two hours of riding, but we can't ride till it's cooler."

"Fine with me," Mark announced. "I wasn't going to ride anyhow, and there aren't enough horses." He gave a frightened glance at Mystery, who was tossing his head and pawing the ground.

"We'll double up on Champagne, Cisco and Cactus Jack," Sophie explained. "You won't have to ride Mystery."

"But if you don't want to get on a horse, we'll leave you out under a nice prickly cactus for the night," Brady offered. "That should give you some protection from the coyotes and cougars."

"He's not serious. He's kidding, right?" Mark's voice rose to a squeal.

"He's partly kidding," Liv said, embarrassed for her brother. "But you might have to suck it up and ride, once the sun sets. We couldn't really leave you out here."

Mark retreated into a surly silence, leaning against the trailer, as far from Mystery as possible. The others hurried to finish getting Cactus Jack, Cisco and Champagne tacked up and out of the blazing sun.

A few steps down the track to the right a grove of wind-whipped pines provided some shade. Liv began tying the horses to the trees with their lead ropes. With every passing second, the sedative was having less effect on Mystery. He struggled against the rope and Liv knew it was still only a tenth of the power in that powerful head and neck.

"Want some help with him?" Brady's tall, gangling frame leaned over her shoulder.

Liv felt a prickle of annoyance, mixed with a wild impulse to throw her arms around his skinny waist and sob on his sturdy shoulder. "I'll be all right," she managed to mumble. "Go help the others."

"Okay, but you've got lots of horses to look after here. Let me take a couple of these lead lines ..." Brady in his eagerness crossed ropes, tripped over a root and lost his footing.

"You are hopeless!" Liv gave him a shove to keep him from sliding into Cisco's side. *Oh well*, she told herself. *As long as Brady is such a clumsy goof, there is no way I'm going to get swept away in a cloud of romance.*

"Sorry!" Brady apologized. "I'm only like this around you. The rest of the time I can at least manage to stay on my feet and be halfway useful." He gave a wry glance at Mark, standing awkwardly in the shade of the trailer at the top of the hill. "But I'm a superhero compared to your brother. Is he always like this?"

Liv stroked Cactus Jack's windblown mane and sighed. "No. I wish you could see Mark at home in Vancouver. He isn't anything like this."

"But what's this crazy idea about not wanting to ride?" Brady still looked puzzled.

"I think he's afraid of horses. And Granddad made such a big thing about riding that he feels bad about being afraid."

"I understand." Brady nodded. "I was terrified of girls until I met you. Afraid to go near them. But you! You were so…" His voice lowered. "Let me just say I had to try no matter how clumsy and scared I was."

Liv laughed. "Lucky for you I was wearing a knee brace after my operation and couldn't get away. Come on, we should finish tying these horses." *So he does like me!* she thought with a burst of happiness. *But what a time to find out, at the top of a hill with a broken down truck and a wild horse coming off his sedative*. One thing you could say about having a crush on somebody; it kept your mind off how much trouble you were in!

She made sure Mystery's rope was tightly tied before they joined Shane, Sophie and Dayna at the trailer. She and Brady were panting from the effort of tying the horses in the heat. What was a fifteen-mile hike leading a wild horse going to feel like?

Together they rifled through Dayna's pickup and horse trailer, tossing trail mix bars, trail mix and wallets in saddlebags, filling canteens with water. "Dayna thought we should go down the right fork," Shane said, hoisting saddlebags over his shoulder as they prepared to set off. "It looks more traveled."

"Let's hope it's the main road," Brady puffed. "We could get awful lost in these hills."

CHAPTER 12
Scorpion

"We've got at least a four hour walk in rough terrain, leading the horses." Dayna glanced at Mark's floppy sneakers. "This desert is crawling with rattlesnakes and poisonous lizards. I know you want to look cool, but you might feel better with something else on your feet."

"Like what?" Mark swiped his hand across his sweaty forehead. His straw hat prickled and his dark shirt and pants drew the heat to his body. He looked like a piece of burnt toast.

Dayna dove into a box of gear stashed in the front compartment of the trailer. "Try these." She pulled out a pair of tall snakeskin boots and held them out to Mark. "They belong to my father." She studied his feet. "They might fit."

"I'm not wearing THOSE!" Mark shoved the boots away. "I am totally against using animal skin to make a pair of stupid cowboy boots." His chin went up. "Besides, I'd look ridiculous."

"You'd look ridiculous with your leg black and rotting from a rattlesnake bite," Dayna shot back. "You're in the desert and until it cools down you have to walk. Try the boots."

"She's right, Mark," Sophie urged. "I got a snake bite when we first came because I was wearing low riding boots. My leg didn't rot because it was a dry bite, but you might not be so lucky."

"Please, Mark," Liv whispered. "Don't act so whiny. "

Mark looked from one sister to the other, dropped his shoulders and sighed. "All right. Give them here."

He took the boots from Dayna's hands, sat on the trailer step, shrugged off his tennis shoes and prepared to pull one on.

"Wait a second!" Shane stepped forward and grabbed the boot.

"What the...?" Mark looked up, his face red with anger and surprise.

"Shake it out first. These boots have been sittin' for a long time." Shane held the boot upside down and shook it vigorously. He handed it back to Mark, who reluctantly pulled it on.

Shane shook the second boot. A red creature the length of his hand flipped out of the boot and scuttled away with its tail arched over its back.

"Scorpion!" Brady shouted. "Good job you didn't step on that. Those things can really hurt. They can even kill a kid."

Mark stared at the scorpion in disbelief. He yanked off the first boot and threw it in Shane's direction. "Keep your stupid boots," he yelled. "I'm sticking to my shoes."

Liv could see that Mark was horribly shaken by his close shave. *Why did it have to be him that almost stepped on a scorpion!* she thought. *Now he'll really be scared of the desert.*

✳ ✳ ✳ ✳ ✳

Twenty minutes later they were far down the track, which twisted and turned like a dog chasing its tail. It grew narrower as they descended. The sand in the road became deeper. Hot wind sweeping up from the desert tore at the shrub oak trees, bending them double.

Shane led Mystery at the head of the group, fighting the wild horse all the way.

"He's never going to hold him," Sophie shouted over the wind to Liv. "I wish we could keep Mystery a little sedated." She and Liv were side-by-side leading Cisco and Cactus Jack.

"Training's better than drugs," Liv yelled back. "I'm sure Mystery *can* be trained, after seeing him with Buck Barnes. If only we get the chance."

Behind them, Brady walked beside Dayna and Champagne. "Dad's going to have a fit about his truck,"

Dayna groaned. "I'm going to have so much explaining to do!"

"But at least you got us away from the coyotes." Brady comforted her. "Things could be a lot worse."

Mark straggled at the end of the line. "I can't see where I'm going in this wind!" he shouted to the others. "The sand blows in my eyes."

"Keep your head down," Dayna roared back at him.

Moments later, Shane's arm was almost torn out of its socket when Mystery jerked back violently. Shane stumbled and stopped.

"What's the matter?" Liv called.

Shane rubbed the grit out of his eyes as he turned to face the others. "The road's washed out. Mystery knew the washout was there before I saw it."

The others edged forward carefully. In front of them, it looked as though a giant earth-moving machine had gouged a wide gash in the dirt road. Its edge was so undercut by the force of rushing water that if Mystery had taken a few more steps it might have crumbled away under his weight.

"It's a long way to the bottom." Liv got down on her knees to look. "We'll never get across with the horses."

Shane was examining the gully. "We can't be on the right road," he muttered. "This trail's been washed out for years."

"What should we do?" Sophie asked above the howling of the wind.

"Go back to the trailer and take the other track," Dayna yelled, turning Champagne. "Can't tell where this one leads – even if we could get across."

"Back to the truck?" Mark had caught up to them in time to realize what they were saying. "You're telling me we took the wrong road? That all this walking has been for nothing?"

"Looks that way," Brady said. "We're just lucky we aren't at the bottom of this gully."

"Thanks to Mystery." Liv handed Brady Cactus Jack's lead rope and stepped forward to stroke Mystery's side. A shiver ran through the stallion. "It's all right, boy," she told him. "I'm just trying to thank you for warning us." Mystery snorted as if to say he could tolerate Liv's touch, as long as she didn't push it!

✳ ✳ ✳ ✳ ✳

The fierce wind was behind them as they climbed back up the hot, dusty track. It was getting late in the day so the hills threw long shadows across their path. In those shadowy patches it was ten degrees cooler.

"There's the Silver Spur truck." Liv caught a flash of red through the chaparral. "Whew! Almost there. We've got to get back before people start to worry."

"Tired?" Brady was at her elbow. "Want me to take a turn leading Cactus Jack?"

"He's no trouble," Liv said. "He's got such good manners – never crowds me or gets in my space."

"Not like me, huh?" Brady grinned.

Liv glanced up to smile at him, but the smile froze on her face. "Brady! Did you see that?"

"What?"

"I thought I saw something moving, near the truck." Liv held up her hand as a warning to the others.

The horses stopped. The only sound was the whistling of the wind near the top of the hill. They moved forward cautiously.

Suddenly there was the crack of a gunshot and loud shouting in Spanish.

"It's the coyotes. They've found the truck. They're shooting at us!" Sophie gasped in terror.

Dayna's face was white. "I don't think they're trying to hit us. They must be mad because the truck blocked the road so they're taking out their frustration on it. Idiots!"

"We're getting out of here, no matter what they're shootin' at." Shane threw himself on Cisco's back and twisted a few turns of Mystery's rope around the saddle horn. He reached out a hand to Sophie. She leaped lightly to the saddle behind him.

Liv turned to face her brother. "C'mon Mark, up on Cactus Jack."

"You said it was too hot to ride!" Mark howled.

"Not in an emergency. You get on in front and I'll do the riding. Grab the saddle horn with both hands." Liv

cupped her hand under Mark's shoe and half tossed him into the saddle.

Behind her Dayna and Brady mounted Champagne.

Liv led the way at a fast trot back down the trail they had climbed moments before, knowing the wind would blow the sound of their riding straight back to the coyotes. With their truck blocked, the two men were on foot. But they had guns.

"What will happen when we get to the washed out part of the road?" Mark's high screech blew back to her.

"Don't know. Have to figure it out ..." Liv realized she'd made a mistake putting Mark in front. He sat in the saddle as stiff as stone, and it was hard to steer.

But there was no time to change positions. The sudden roar of an engine put the four horses in flight.

CHAPTER 13
Where is Champagne?

Liv let Cactus Jack run on a loose rein. Mark gripped the saddle horn with all his might. "They must have brought an all-terrain vehicle in the back of the pickup," she yelled up to him. "They were ready for anything!" *It's a good thing the road was so twisty*, she thought. *On a straightaway we'd be easy to catch with an ATV.*

She and Cactus Jack were still in the lead. Liv had a sudden inspiration. "Follow me," she shouted over her shoulder, "and spread out!" She plunged Cactus Jack toward the bushes at the side of the road. He dove into the tangle of mesquite and manzanita.

"What are you doing?" Mark screeched. "We're going to die."

"Keep your head down," Liv yelled at him. "Lean forward and grab Jack's mane with both hands."

They crashed through the brush, at an angle to the road. It would be suicide for the coyotes to chase them through this on their ATV. Cactus Jack could dodge and twist and find his way through the thickest chaparral. He'd been bred to flush stray cows out of a mess of brush like this.

The washout, when they reached it, was wider and shallower than at the road. Vegetation had kept the rushing water from carving a steep-sided gully. "Lean back!" Liv shouted to Mark as Cactus Jack pitched down its side.

She stopped at the bottom, sure they were hidden from above by a screen of live oak. Cactus Jack, sides heaving, stood waiting for the others. Seconds later Cisco clattered down the loose gravel beside him with Shane and Sophie on his back. His coat was caked white with sweat.

"I lost Mystery," Shane panted. "Yanked the rope so hard I thought the saddle might come off."

"You couldn't help it," Liv puffed. "I know that."

"Where are Brady and Dayna?" Sophie looked up the side of the gully.

They all stared at each other, breathless. "Did anyone see Champagne, or hear her?" Liv asked in a trembling voice. Champagne was a show horse, not used to dodging through thick brush.

None of them had.

They listened for the sound of the ATV but everything was quiet. Then, in the distance, they heard a high neigh of distress. "That's Champagne!" Sophie cried. "I'm sure it is."

"The coyotes must have her," Liv groaned. "It's my fault. I should have known Champagne would be too scared to follow us off the trail. She's spent her whole life in corrals and riding rings."

"Do you think that means they've got Brady and Dayna?" Sophie asked, her voice shaking.

Shane's face was grim. "They might. I doubt Dayna would leave her mare."

Liv nodded. "I'm sure she wouldn't. And Brady wouldn't leave Dayna."

"Now what?" Mark was still clinging desperately to Cactus Jack's mane. "Do you guys realize what you risked for that crazy black horse? Dayna and Brady are probably prisoners. And now you've lost Mystery, too."

Shane ignored this outburst. "We need to get out of this gully," he said firmly, dismounting and helping Sophie down. He stood with his arm around her waist, unconsciously steadying her against him. "We can't do anything down here."

"We could stay out of sight till dark, sneak away and head back to civilization," Mark suggested, sarcasm burning in his voice.

Liv reached forward and pried Mark's fingers loose from their grip on Cactus Jack's mane. "Sophie, help me get Mark off," she said.

Sophie slipped out of Shane's embrace. Too late she reached for her brother. Mark tried to dismount by himself, and fell in a heap. He scrambled out of reach of the horse's hoofs.

"Ow!" he howled, rubbing his shin.

"Maybe you *should* just stay here while the rest of us try to help our friends," Sophie told Mark. She had tried to hold onto her faith in her big brother but it was crumbling.

"Dayna and Brady need more than you three idiots." Mark kept rubbing his sore leg. "We need the police, the sheriff, whoever. We can't do anything by ourselves against guys with guns."

"We're wasting precious time." Shane slammed his hat down tight. "Let's try to circle around the truck and trailer – see if we can find out where Dayna and Brady are. We'll keep the horses with us."

Mark grunted, "You're all completely insane!" But he clambered to his feet and limped after them as they headed out of the gully.

"Watch out for rattlesnakes," Liv warned Mark. "You might not hear the rattle in this wind." She could see he was paying the price for not wearing boots. His jeans and canvas sneakers were snagged by every thorn bush and cactus he passed.

"Are you just trying to scare me?" Mark stopped dead.

"Come on, Mark, you saw the scorpion. There are real live rattlesnakes, too."

"What do they look like?"

"They're brown and white with diamond-shaped markings," Liv told him. "It's still too hot for them to be out, but watch the shady patches." The slant of the afternoon sun had given every rock and bush a shadow.

Mark started moving again, picking up each foot carefully.

"Not that slow. We're getting behind," said Liv, urging Cactus Jack forward.

"You think I'm hopeless, don't you? You'd be glad if I got bit by a snake." Mark groaned. "You care a lot more about that Brady guy than me."

It was Liv's turn to stop. "To be honest, Mark, I *am* more worried about Brady and Dayna right now than you." She wanted to punch her brother at that moment. "And I'll tell you something else. If things were the other way around, and you were in trouble, Brady Bolt would do anything to help you!"

"Oh, sure!" was all Mark said, but Liv knew she'd hit a nerve. He started walking faster and soon they had caught up to Shane, Sophie and Cisco.

"I'm gonna get around Dayna's rig – see if the coyotes' vehicle is still there or if they've gone," Shane said.

"Gone?" Sophie looked up at him.

Shane pulled his hat down to his eyebrows, the way he always did when he was worried. "They've got a trailer," he reminded Sophie. "They could have loaded Champagne and taken off."

"That would be horsenapping!" Liv exclaimed.

"I'm not saying they did," said Shane. "But it's a possibility. We haven't heard anything in a while."

"They might be waiting for us," Mark murmured. "An ambush…"

"That's a possibility too," Shane admitted. "You three stay here with the horses and I'll scout it out."

"I'm coming with you!" Liv insisted.

"Me too," Sophie joined in. "Mark, why don't you stay here, where it's safe."

"I'm not staying with horses." Mark hunched up his shoulders.

"Suit yourself." Sophie's patience had worn paper-thin. She looped Cisco's rope around a twisted oak branch.

Liv tied Cactus Jack beside him and stroked his long nose. "You guys be quiet, now. Don't give us away."

"Leave them loose tied," said Shane. "In case we don't make it back, they'll be able to get free."

"Great!" grumbled Mark. "You think of everything." The two sixteen-year olds glared at each other. Shane would have said something, but rescuing Brady, Dayna and Champagne was more important now.

CHAPTER 14
Captured!

Locked in the coyotes' horse trailer, Dayna twisted in misery. "If we only had a phone to call for help," she groaned. "I'm worried about Champagne. Those guys treated her so roughly, and look what they did to my father's precious truck – shot out all four tires!"

"I'm broiling," Brady swiped the sweat off his brow. "I wonder how long they're going to keep us here."

The short, smelly horse trailer held the stink of all the terrified horses the horse smugglers had hauled. Dayna peered out the ventilation slats in its side.

"What are they doing out there?" Brady asked.

"I can't tell. I can't see anything except trees and bushes. No sign of the coyotes. They're probably arguing about what to do with us." Dayna sighed and slumped to the trailer floor beside Brady. "I think we'll have a long wait."

"Do you think the others got away?"

Dayna gave a tiny shrug. "They must have. But if they did they'll come back for us. Shane's a tough cowboy and Liv is nuts about you."

"Do you think so?" Brady frowned. "I thought we had something going, but now she just teases me all the time."

"Have you kissed her?"

"Huh!" Brady squirmed uncomfortably. "I tried, once, but I stepped in a water bucket and sort of ... fell into her."

"Very romantic."

"Why are we talking about this when we're about to be shot or kidnapped?" Brady got to his feet, blushing.

"Might as well talk about something." Dayna shrugged again.

"Okay. You're right. We'll talk about our friends." Brady tried to grin. "How is Temo? Did you have a nice visit?"

It was Dayna's turn to blush. "Yes, we had a very nice visit. He was glad to get his horse back." Her voice sank. "The trouble is, I don't know when I'll see him again. I don't have anything else to return to him."

"I'm sure," Brady said sincerely, "that Helado was just an excuse to see you."

Dayna sighed. "You didn't watch the way his eyes lit up when ..."

She never finished. The front trailer door burst open with a bang. The two coyotes stood in the opening.

"What have you done with my mare?" Dayna demanded to know.

The man who spoke better English waved off her question. "First things first. We have spotted your friends on the ridge. Perhaps they are coming to rescue you." He gave a short laugh. "So we will prepare a nice welcome for them. Come out."

"You can't use *us* to trap our friends," Dayna said furiously. "We'll shout and warn them!"

"Then we'll shoot your horse." The man glared at her. "Is that what you want?"

"If you hurt one hair on Champagne's head you'll wish you'd never been born!" Dayna's eyes were on fire. She stood facing the coyotes with her hands on her hips.

The man who did the talking said slowly, "We only want the black horse we have worked so hard to capture. Your friends have taken him from us – not once, but twice. Give him back and you and your pretty mare go free."

Dayna and Brady didn't dare look at each other. They'd both seen Mystery tear himself free only seconds before they lost sight of Shane. It would be impossible to trade Champagne for the stallion – he was gone.

The coyote moved away from the open door and motioned them forward.

Dayna began shouting. "SHANE! LIV! WE'RE IN HERE ..." as she got to the door.

Brady clapped a hand over her mouth before she could finish. "Quiet!"

"Smart boy." The coyote grinned. "Keep her quiet."

Brady wrestled a struggling Dayna through the door and outside. "Brady … what are you DOING?" her muffled voice came through his fingers.

"Calm down," Brady muttered. He had seen the look in the coyote's eyes. They were cold and blank. Brady's family raised bulls for the rodeo, for the bull riding events. The bulls that were really bad, the mean ruthless killers, all had the look of that man. Brady knew they were in serious danger and Dayna's fearless resistance could only make it worse.

❊ ❊ ❊ ❊ ❊

From the top of the ridge, Liv, Sophie, Shane and Mark looked down at the crowded road below. The coyotes' truck was tight against Dayna's long Silver Spur rig. The front door of the trailer was on the other side, facing away from them. They could hear voices, but couldn't see Champagne, Brady or Dayna.

"Do you think they've seen us?" Liv whispered to Shane.

"Might have. Keep down!" Shane shot a furious glance at Mark, who had gotten stiff lying still and was trying to change positions.

Mark made a sour face at Shane and then flattened on his belly and slid backwards until he was far enough down the ridge to stand up.

"Where are you going?" Sophie tried to keep her voice down. "Mark!"

"Somewhere away from you guys – as far as possible!" He waved a dismissive hand and started off through the thick brush.

"Sophie, go after him," Liv hissed. "We can't let him get lost."

Why not you? Sophie gulped back the angry words. She wanted to stay with Shane, not go after her brother like some kind of babysitter! Once she had loved Mark for the way he stuck up for her when Liv got too bossy. Now he was a like a little kid, putting them all in greater danger. But even as she thought this, Sophie knew it was right that Liv stayed with Shane. When it came to taking action, her twin was braver and stronger than she was.

She slipped down the gravelly slope after Mark.

He barely glanced back as she caught up with him. "Why don't you stay up there with your boyfriend?"

"I've told you before, he's not my boyfriend. Shane's like a brother to me."

Mark whipped around. "You don't need a brother," he growled. "You already have one, in case you don't remember."

"This is a stupid time to get jealous of Shane." Sophie tried to keep her voice level. "We've got to find where the coyotes are keeping Dayna and Brady and try to help them."

"I could help," Mark spat out the words, "if we were back on the mountains in British Colombia. I'd like to see Shane in his stupid high-heeled boots in the snow. I'll bet he'd fall and freeze his rear end –"

"Stop that!" Sophie blazed. "I'm sure Shane can't ski, and he can't skate and he'd be useless in deep snow. But if we were in a blizzard and there was an emergency, *he'd* try his best, without complaining about how tough it was. That's all I'm asking you to do. Stop acting like a jerk. Be nice!"

There were tears in Mark's eyes as he gazed at her. "Everybody's been telling me that since Dad left. 'Be nice, be nice, be nice.' I can't be nice, I'm too mad! I wish we were back in Vancouver right now!"

"I know you do. And you'll likely get your way. After this, Mom's going to pack us all up and leave the ranch. It will break Liv's heart."

"But not yours?" Mark gulped.

"I won't mind going back," Sophie admitted. "I miss the big trees, and the green and the ocean back home. But if I had to, I'd still choose the ranch. I love Gran and Granddad, and the horses."

By this time they had reached the place where Cisco and Cactus Jack were tied. Mark stood nervously out of the way while Sophie petted and soothed the two horses, telling them how wonderful and quiet they were and how much she loved them.

Cisco put his big white face in the center of her chest and blew softly.

"See, they're not dangerous." Sophie spoke softly over her shoulder to Mark. "Come and rub Cisco between his ears. He likes that."

Mark stepped cautiously forward. Cisco let him scrub the area between his ears for a moment. Then his head shot up.

Mark nearly fell backwards. "What did I do?" he cried. "Horses hate me."

"It's not you. Look at Cactus Jack." Jack wheeled on his rope, ready to kick out.

Sophie had to work to control them. "Something's got them riled up." She took a shorter grip on Cisco's lead rope. "Something's out there in the bush. Could be a cougar!"

CHAPTER 15
Horse Trading

Sophie had seen what a cougar could do to a horse. Granddad's lead mare Carmelita had been torn to pieces fighting a cougar. She'd managed to save her foal Bando, but lost her life. Sophie didn't dare describe that horrible scene to Mark.

"A cougar?" Mark asked anxiously. "Is that the same as a mountain lion?"

Sophie nodded. "Same thing. Sh-sh!" She listened intently to the sounds in the brush. "I don't think it can be a cougar," she said softly. "It's making too much noise. But it's a big animal."

She looked carefully at Cactus Jack and Cisco. Instead of getting more agitated, the two horses were settling down.

"Look at them," she whispered to Mark. "They were startled, but they're not afraid. I think it must be the mystery stallion out there. He's looking for Champagne."

"Why would he come back for Champagne when he had his freedom?" Mark peered into the brush. He could see nothing but gray-brown leaves and cactus plants.

"You really don't know anything about horses, do you?" Sophie said. "Mystery wants Champagne because she's a mare and that's what stallions do. They round up mares. That's why he's always in trouble with ranchers like Granddad and Dayna's father. He drives off their mares and fights their stallions."

"I know how Mystery feels," Mark said. "No good for anything and always in everybody's way!"

"You're not ..." Sophie began, but there was so much truth in what Mark said that she couldn't finish.

"Why don't these horses act like Mystery?" Mark motioned to Cactus Jack and Cisco.

"Because they're geldings. They've been neutered, like our old dog Skipper, so they can't reproduce."

"Oh." Mark said. "So Mystery would be a good fighting horse, and that's why the coyotes want him."

"You've got it," sighed Sophie. "Liv thinks he can be trained."

"Maybe," Mark said. "I saw how Buck Barnes had him almost eating out of his hand. I wonder what the stallion will do now?"

"If he's smart, he'll keep running," Sophie said sadly.

"But I'm afraid he's not that smart." She paused, studying Mark with her head to one side. "Hey, how about a second riding lesson?"

"No, uh-uh. No way." Mark backed up, tripped on a root and sat down on a prickly bush. "Ow! No." He scrambled to his feet. "You're not getting me back on him." He pointed to Cactus Jack.

"Listen to me," Sophie went on. "You can't walk in the desert. I've tried and it was terrible. Besides the snakes and scorpions there are poisonous lizards called Gila Monsters and horrible pig-like animals called javelinas that attack in herds. You just have to ride." *I'm exaggerating about the javelinas, but I can't leave Mark alone here on foot*, Sophie thought, *and I can't stay here when Liv and the others need help*.

She glanced up at the sky. "It's hazy and getting late. It's cool enough to ride, or will be soon."

"I can't. I fell off, remember?"

"People fall off all the time. They say you have to fall off a horse a hundred times to be a good rider."

Mark groaned and rolled his eyes.

"Anyway, I'm going to show you how to *not* fall off," Sophie rushed on. "Remember learning to ski? The first thing they teach you is how to stop. I'll show you how to stop Cisco."

"Cisco? Not Cactus Jack?" Mark was picking thorns out of his pants.

"Cactus Jack will remember the last time you tried to ride. Horses never forget."

Mark shuddered. "Neither do I!"

"Don't worry. Cisco is steadier and gentler. Stand on that rock over there so you won't yank his saddle getting on." Sophie pointed to a large, flat-topped boulder.

"He'll know I'm afraid. I can't hide it." Mark shrugged. "Face it, Sophie, I'm not the cowboy type."

"Sure you are. You're descended from a long line of Spanish-American cowboys, just like me and Liv. Gran told us. We're all members of the Lopez family that brought these horses to Arizona a long time ago."

"You're making this up!' Mark scoffed. "I never heard anything about being descended from cowboys!"

"That's because Dad didn't want us to know and I guess Mom wanted to stay married so she never told us either. But it's true. We don't have time now, but I'll tell you all about it someday. Right now, I want you to channel your Mexican ancestors …"

"The horse isn't going to buy this ancestor stuff," Mark protested. "He's still going to know I'm scared."

"I agree," said Sophie. "So talk to him. Tell Cisco exactly what you feel. He'll know anyway and that way he won't be getting a mixed message – your voice saying one thing and your body another. That confuses him and makes him think there's something to be nervous about."

Mark looked doubtful, but he climbed on the rock anyway.

"Go on, talk to him. And at the same time take these reins and hold them like this." Sophie showed him. "I'll hold his head so he doesn't move."

"All right." Mark took a deep breath. "I'm scared witless," he told Cisco, "but I know Sophie's right. I have to ride to help Liv and Dayna and the guys. Sophie and I are like the ski patrol in a storm. You're my transportation."

He gripped the reins and Cisco's mane in his left hand, put his foot in the stirrup and managed to swing his right leg over the saddle. "So you're okay with me sitting up here on your back, right?"

❋ ❋ ❋ ❋ ❋

"Come down from there!" The English-speaking coyote pointed to Liv and Shane on the ridge above the road. "We see you and we have your friends."

As they half-slid, half-ran down the ridge, Liv whispered to Shane, "I'm glad Mark and Sophie got away. Hope the coyotes don't notice they've gone."

On the far side of the small trailer, Brady and Dayna, their faces smudged with dirt, greeted them with relief. Liv was so glad to see them alive and unharmed that she couldn't hold back a huge grin.

Sophie? Dayna's eyes signaled the question. *And Mark?*

Liv tried to reassure her. "*Everybody's* okay, but where's Champagne?"

"You will get the palomino when we get our black stallion," the man growled. "What have you done with him?"

"So that's what you're after," Shane spoke quickly. "He's up there a little way, where the road is washed out." He pointed to the road to the left.

You can't tell he's bluffing. Liv gave Shane an admiring glance. *He has no idea where Mystery is, or even if that road is washed out. We've never been up that way.*

"How is the horse? Still drugged?" The smuggler's eyebrow twitched nervously. He'd had a bad experience with a dangerously wide-awake Mystery.

"Yes, poor horse! He's pretty sluggish from whatever you gave him," Liv said indignantly, playing along with Shane's bluff. If the coyotes found out they'd lost Mystery they'd be in real trouble!

"We will go and pick him up. We will stop at the washout."

Dayna said. "Please, tell me where you've got Champagne."

"In there," grunted the coyote with a quick jab of his finger toward Dayna's trailer.

Dayna's eyes widened in horror. "You've got to let her out before she dies of the heat."

The man considered. "I suppose a dead horse is not much good for horse trading, eh?" He laughed a coarse laugh. "All right. Carlos, bring out the mare."

Liv held her breath as the trailer door swung open. The shadow of the ridge above the road had shaded the trailer, keeping it cooler, but for how long? There was no whinny from inside the large, hollow space.

Dayna was already running.

"Hold it. She is not yours, yet." The coyote stepped in front of Dayna.

"Let her go!" Liv dashed forward to help her friend. The second man, stockier and taller, started toward her.

Brady moved quickly between them and put his arm around Liv. His square face, under the brim of his cowboy hat, was more serious than she had ever seen it. "Back off," he warned in an urgent whisper. "Don't push these men. We'll get our chance, but not now. Trust me."

"All right," Liv gulped.

The second man moved into the trailer. There was the metallic clang of stall bars coming down, the clop of hoofs on rubber matting and Champagne appeared in the doorway.

"She needs water!" Dayna begged, "Let me go."

The first coyote loosened his hold and Dayna sped to lead her mare down the ramp. Luckily Champagne hadn't been shut in the trailer long enough to do serious damage, but when Dayna pinched a fold of skin it stayed in a tent too long. She was dehydrated from the heat.

Shane helped drain a couple of water containers into a

bucket and they all stood in the sunlit road, watching the golden horse drink.

Suddenly the second man said something to the first in Spanish. He jolted, stared at the four teens and spoke harshly. "My *amigo* says he saw six of you kids back at Fort Parson. He wants to know where are the other two?" His eyes gleamed with suspicion. "And where are your horses? You had better tell us the truth."

Liv threw up her hands and raised her eyebrows. "Who knows? But they can't have gone far. My brother is afraid to ride." *That part at least, was true.*

"So we find them later. Right now we go and get the stallion." He snarled the order to Dayna, "Move your truck, *senorita*. Even with holes in the tires, you can drive it out of the way."

CHAPTER 16
Another Lesson

The two coyotes were furious to find that the red pickup's engine refused to start.

"It didn't help that you shot out the tires," Dayna couldn't resist pointing out.

Brady shot her a warning glance. The two men were getting more and more frustrated. It was dangerous to remind them of their guns.

The silent coyote patted the ATV standing near their own truck and muttered something in Spanish.

"No, Carlos, we can't use the ATV. We need our *camion* to pick up the stallion." The English-speaking smuggler turned his furious gaze on Dayna. "We will have to push your useless pickup out of the way. Then we can squeeze ours past the trailer."

He pointed to the others. "You all help push," he grunted. "Push hard, or the mare will feel my anger."

He pointed to Champagne, who was grazing under an oak tree.

With the trailer unhooked and six of them pushing, the Silver Spur truck was shoved to the side. Champagne was loaded in the small, stinking trailer. Liv, Brady, Shane and Dayna were shoved in with her, and the rear door slammed shut.

The trailer was stifling and crowded with a large horse and four people. Brady jolted into Liv as they jerked onto the main road. "We have to stop running into each other like this," he tried to joke, wrapping his arms around her.

Liv made a face, but hugged him hard.

"Shane, what are we going to do," Dayna asked, almost crying, "when they find out Mystery is gone?"

✳ ✳ ✳ ✳ ✳

Not far from there, in the shady spot where they had tied the horses, Mark perched on Cisco's back as rigid as a toy action figure. His hands gripped the reins like a lifeline, and his feet were frozen in the stirrups.

Sophie thought fast. How could she shrink years of riding lessons into one all-important one? *Don't tell Mark too much all at once. He'll get confused and tense up even more!*

"Shoulders down, chest up," she told him. "That's right, take a deep breath." She could see Mark relax and Cisco, reacting, took a deep breath too. *Good start!* "Don't squeeze the reins," she went on. "Hold them like they were a little animal – like a gerbil – that you don't want to squish."

She showed him how to steer Cisco by moving the reins left and right. "And if you lose your balance, don't pull on the reins. Grab his mane, or the saddle horn. That way you aren't yanking on the bit in his mouth."

"You were going to show me how to stop." Mark said. The frozen look had left his face but he looked very vulnerable sitting up there.

"The easiest way," Sophie explained, "is just to sit back, sit deep and think, 'Stop.' You can say 'Whoa,' too."

"How does the horse know what I'm thinking? He can't read minds."

"No, but he can read your body," Sophie promised. "It's visualization, like in any sport. If you picture stopping, your body will mirror the thought and Cisco will pick it up." She hugged Cisco around his neck and whispered in his ear, "Please, Cisco, look after my big brother."

They were out of time. "Let's go," Sophie urged. She mounted Cactus Jack in one quick motion and gave him the signal to move off. "Give him a little cluck," she called back to Mark. "He'll follow."

Behind her, Mark clucked and Cisco took a few steps. Mark practiced stopping. To his surprise, Cisco seemed to know exactly what he meant without pulling on the reins. *Stop. Go. Stop. Go.* It worked!

They rode through the trees to the main road, hoping to circle back to the ridge that overlooked the fork.

Mark was surprised at the way Cisco picked his way through the thorn bushes, knowing exactly where to place his feet on the stony ground. How did the horse do that? Riding above the thorns was much easier than walking and you could see so much better from Cisco's back.

"Mark! Hold up!" Sophie had stopped ahead of him. "Listen."

"Is it the ATV again?" Mark rode Cisco up beside her.

"No, it's a truck. Look, we're almost at the road and it's coming toward us." Sophie held back the branch so he could see.

"Mark, it's the coyotes' truck," she gasped. "There's a horse inside – I can see through the slats – it's Champagne. And people! I think it's Liv and Brady."

"Did they see you?" Mark asked.

"No, the coyotes would have stopped if they'd seen us." The trailer had disappeared around a bend. Sophie urged Cactus Jack forward onto the dirt road.

"What now?" Mark followed her on Cisco. "We can't keep up with a truck."

"It's not going very fast and they might stop somewhere," Sophie said quickly. "Do you think you could ride a little faster?"

"I … don't know," muttered Mark.

"Just think, one two, three four, the rhythm of Cisco's

feet," Sophie told him. "Let your body relax into the rhythm." She sped up on Cactus Jack and turned to look at Mark. The expression on his face was almost comical. Apart from a slight bouncing in the saddle, he was jogging along on a loose rein.

Liv was right, Sophie thought, astonished. *Our brother's a natural.*

❊ ❊ ❊ ❊ ❊

Dayna peered out the slats in the trailer side. "Shouldn't we hit the washout soon?"

Shane joined her at the ventilation slats. He squinted at the sky. "It looks like the road's headin' west," he said. "Might not be washed out at all over here."

At that moment the trailer slewed wildly to one side. They'd stopped.

The front door was wrenched open. "Out!" the English-speaking coyote ordered. "Where's the horse? *Donde esta el caballo?*" His brows were knotted in anger.

CHAPTER 17
Tricked!

"I ask you again. Where is the horse?" The hot wind blew dust in their faces as Dayna, Brady, Liv and Shane squirmed out of the front of the trailer. This road had taken them higher into the Ocotillo Hills.

"There is no washout here!" The angry man's words gusted at them like the wind itself. "There could be no water this high. You have tried to fool us!"

The sky had turned slate gray. Champagne snorted and pawed at the trailer floor, anxious to be set free.

"What have you done with the stallion?" The coyote's words rose to a shout above the wailing wind.

"We haven't done anything with him." Liv stepped forward bravely. "He escaped, that's all. The drug wore off and we couldn't hold him."

"You lied. And you are still lying …" The man came to meet her, his hand upstretched.

Brady spoke up. "She's not lying. That's what happened. The stallion got away, like he did before. He's too strong."

The coyote spun around in fury. He spoke in a low, urgent voice to his partner. They both nodded. "Get back in the trailer," the spokesman ordered, "with the mare. She is worth something, a fine palomino like that. We decide what to do with you later on."

Dayna opened her mouth to protest, but a warning look from the others stopped her. Shane and Brady hurried her into the trailer where she stood by Champagne's head, soothing the worried mare. "It's all right," she murmured. "I'd never let men like that take you."

The coyotes' truck rumbled to life again and the trailer jolted forward. Liv and Brady exchanged a glance. *Where were they going now?*

✳ ✳ ✳ ✳ ✳

Sophie and Mark were just in time to see the truck and trailer start up the hill.

"We almost caught up," Mark panted in frustration. "Can't we go faster? I think I'm really getting the hang of riding."

"You are, but we can't press the horses any harder. The wind is stronger and the road is heading uphill." Sophie leaned forward to stroke Cactus Jack's sweaty neck.

"But it's cooler!" Mark swiped the sweat off his forehead. "Look! The sky's all black over there. The sun's behind those clouds. We have to keep going. Maybe the truck will stop again and we'll have a chance ..."

"In a minute." Sophie reached back for the canteen of water in her saddlebag and handed it to her brother. "Here, Mark, drink. It's important to take in enough water. Helps keep your mind clear."

Mark nodded and reached for the canteen. "Like keeping warm in a blizzard." He took a few big gulps. "Extreme conditions – I get it." He patted Cisco's neck cautiously. "How about the horses? Don't they need to drink?"

"Of course they do – and soon," Sophie told him. "I hope those clouds mean a thunder storm and we'll get some water on the ground."

"Doesn't that usually happen in a thunder storm?"

"Not here." Sophie shook her head. "Lots of times the rain never reaches the ground."

"Ugh! Desert!" Mark muttered. "Let's get going. I can tell Cisco's tired of waiting around."

"Okay." Sophie reached for her canteen and swallowed a few mouthfuls of water herself. Despite the weight of worry on her shoulders, she felt a spurt of relief. Mark was talking, interested in what was going on – almost like his old self. There was an eager look on his face as he started after the disappearing truck. It was as if riding Cisco had brought him back to life. She threw her horse a grateful glance. *Mark thinks he's in charge, but it's really you that's making it happen.*

＊ ＊ ＊ ＊ ＊

At the top of the Ocotillo Hills a small chopper hovered above Dayna's truck and trailer. "Hey!" the pilot shouted over the noise of the spinning blades. "Somebody's big horse rig's down there on the road. What's it doing away up here?"

"Should we set down and take a look?" His passenger trained binoculars on the Silver Spur truck.

"I don't see anybody. The weather's not looking good, and we're due back in Tucson in half an hour," the pilot reminded him. "Maybe it's an old wreck – maybe been sittin' there for a long time. Things in the desert don't weather much." He and his passenger, a mining engineer, were scouting the Ocotillo Hills for a likely spot to prospect for silver.

"Maybe." The engineer put down his glasses. "But it's a horse trailer. My daughter Lucy's crazy about horses. If she was here she'd want us to land and check it out."

"You're the boss." The pilot circled the top of the hill, checking for a flat spot to land the helicopter. He set it down on the ridge as gently as a dragonfly on a leaf.

The two men ducked under the spinning blades. They slid down the ridge to the truck.

"Hank!" the engineer exclaimed, "Look at this! Somebody shot out all the tires on the pickup."

"This is no old wreck." The pilot read the name on the truck. "Silver Spur – that's a fancy dude ranch near Rattlesnake Bend. See if anything's inside the trailer."

125

The engineer checked inside. "Whew! You're right," he said. "The horse buns are nice and fresh in here. I'd say just hours old. Wonder what happened to the driver and the horse, or horses?"

"Let's go up again and take a look around," the pilot suggested, "and at the same time I'll radio the police to get in touch with the ranch. I don't like the looks of this."

The helicopter soared into the air. To the north, where the desert floor was as flat as a frying pan, bolts of lightning streaked the black clouds.

"Hey, Hank! What on earth is that?" The engineer pointed to a cloud that stretched to the desert floor. It was triangular in shape, a dusky red color and moving.

"Jumping catfish! That, my friend, is a sandstorm – about a mile high and coming right at us." The pilot pointed to the cloud. "We don't get many sandstorms, but when we do, they're killers. This one is moving fast."

He checked his radio. It was a blur of static. "I guess I won't be sending any messages to the Silver Spur ranch," the pilot said grimly. "I'm headin' south, away from that monster. The last sandstorm around here crashed one of our choppers near Tucson."

He tipped the steering toward the south and stared at the vanishing Ocotillo Hills. "Man! I sure hope there isn't anybody on the ground in the path of that sandstorm!"

CHAPTER 18
Visibility – Zero

"Look, Sophie, a helicopter." Mark squinted at the sky. "We're saved! They'll see us and send for help."

Sophie glanced over her shoulder at the circling chopper. She waved frantically but without much hope that whoever was in the helicopter would see them. The chopper was headed in the opposite direction.

She and Mark had reached the top of the pass. From there they looked out over the flat desert to the mountains in the distance. Now they could see the flashes of lightning more clearly. Against the inky black sky, a huge red cloud bulged from the clouds to the ground.

"What is that?" Mark yelled, pointing to the cloud in astonishment.

"I have no idea," she shouted back. "But it doesn't look like rain." *Is this some new desert disaster?* she gasped to herself.

Cactus Jack and Cisco snorted and shook their heads as if they could tell her about the danger if they could talk.

"I can't see the coyotes' truck and trailer," Mark called from behind her. "Can you?"

"No, but the road's like a corkscrew – steep and zig-zaggy all the way down. They might not be too far ahead." Sophie gathered Cactus Jack's reins. "Listen, Mark. I want you to lean back to help Cisco on the steep parts of the hill – like this." She leaned back in the saddle to show Mark what she meant.

"I know," Mark told her. "Liv already showed me that."

✳ ✳ ✳ ✳ ✳

In the jolting suffocating trailer, Liv and the others could not hear the rattle of the helicopter blades, or see the sky. They were bucketing down the other side of the Ocotillo Hills.

"The road's even worse on this side of the hills!" gasped Dayna, holding onto a stall bar to keep herself from pitching forward. The truck swung around a curve, sending them all pitching around the inside of the smelly trailer.

"Oh, poor baby!" Dayna tried to steady Champagne in her stall, hoping the rough ride in this rattletrap trailer wouldn't injure her mare.

On the next sharp curve Liv was thrown violently against Brady. "Hey!" he cried, holding her tightly. "This time *you* crashed into *me*!"

"Why are they taking these corners so fast?" Liv

pushed herself away. "I feel like any second we're going to go flying off a cliff!"

Shane strained to see out the ventilation slats. "Something's goin' on out there," he said, glancing at his watch. "It's too early to be this dark."

Five minutes later they were all fighting for breath.

"What's happening?" Liv choked. "Shane, what can you see?"

"Nothing. It's all black ... it's ... a sandstorm!" he shouted. "The driver must have been tryin' to outrun it. Quick! Cover your faces."

The air in the trailer, which had been hot and stifling, was filling fast with fine sand. Champagne whinnied her distress. Shane pulled the bandanna he wore around his neck up over his mouth and nose. Dayna tied her scarf the same way. Brady whipped off his own bandanna and tied it around Liv's face. He pulled the collar of his shirt up over his own. They all struggled to breathe.

The truck slewed wildly from side to side for a terrifying moment as the trailer jack-knifed. Then they felt and heard a CRASH that threw them to the trailer floor. After that, there was only the shrieking of the wind and sand hurled against the trailer's metal sides.

"Champagne!" Liv heard Dayna's choked cry, "Baby, are you all right?"

At that second the rear door of the trailer was wrenched open.

Liv froze against Brady, expecting the coyotes to leap into the small space on top of them.

Instead she heard a much-loved voice shouting above the wind. "LIV! ARE YOU IN THERE?"

"Mark!" Liv shot forward in the howling darkness, into her brother's arms.

"Come on!" They heard Sophie's muffled order. "Bring Champagne out. We've got to get on the horses and get away."

Brady, Liv and Shane leaped from the back of the trailer into the stinging sandstorm. Dayna came last, leading her mare.

"Here!" Liv felt Cactus Jack's reins thrust into her hand. "You and Brady ride Jack. Mark and I will ride Cisco. Is Champagne all right, Dayna?" Sophie choked.

"I ... think so," Dayna's voice came faintly out of the swirling dust.

Liv knew it was mere seconds before the two men in the cab of the truck would be after them, unless the crash had injured them badly. "Do you think we should check on the coyotes?" she gasped to Brady.

"Not now!" Brady was already on Cactus Jack. He leaned over, grabbed her arm and hauled her up behind him. "They still have a gun."

"Which way?" Liv croaked out the question.

"Let the horses have their heads." She heard Shane's

voice. "This will blow over soon. We want to get as far away as we can."

Visibility was zero, but Liv could tell they were near the desert flats, with no shelter from the tearing, searing sand. There were no trees and only scattered bushes. Soon the horses stopped, turned their backs to the wind and stood close together.

"It's no use," Brady howled. "They won't move. We'll have to get off and lead them."

The sand blew under their face scarves, into their mouths and noses. Leading Cactus Jack, Liv reached for Sophie's hand in the blast of sand. "You and Mark saved us," she managed to scream above the wind. "I was so glad it was *you* when that trailer door opened."

"We're not saved, yet," Sophie yelled in her ear, "but Mark's good. He's –"

"I'm here, little sisters." Mark was suddenly beside them. "Let me lead Cisco for you."

"If we could just SEE!" Liv cried. "We have no idea if we're going back toward the coyotes or away from them."

"Then we should stop." Sophie handed her lead rope to Mark and sank to her knees, shielding her head from the storm.

A blaring blast of a horn brought them straight upright. Liv turned to see blurred blobs of light bobbing toward her. "The coyotes," she tried to shout. Sand filled her mouth and she spat furiously.

CHAPTER 19
Sandstorm

The coyotes' pickup with its trailer was coming directly at them across the open desert. The horses stood like statues in sheets of blowing sand. In the height of the storm there was no escape.

At that moment a large warm shape swirled out of the dust. Liv heard a high whicker, and suddenly the black horse was close and urgent, pressing against the other horses, nipping at their flanks, urging them away from the truck lights.

"Mystery!" Liv tried to cry. *Of course he must have been following the horses since he tore the rope from Shane's hand*, she thought, *watching, waiting for another chance to round up Champagne*. The lead rope dangled dangerously from his halter. Sooner or later he would step on it, or get it tangled in some brush and injure himself. Now he just shook his great black head as the horses surged forward in response to his command.

Liv clung to Cactus Jack's neck. She felt a terrifying sinking. The ground fell away at her feet. She was slipping, Cactus Jack lurching downward. Mystery had led them over the lip of a gulch. There was no way to tell how deep it was or how steep the sides. It was like falling in a dream, with the red sand making it impossible to see.

To Liv's relief the gulch was not deep – not much more than twice her height. At the bottom was shelter from the storm. Mystery had known exactly what he was doing. He had herded them all into a windbreak. Now they could see each other's shocked, storm-battered faces, and the horses. There was Mystery, his proud neck arched over Champagne's.

"Hold your mare tight," Shane shouted to Dayna. "He'll try to cut her out and run her off. That's what he wants."

"Help!" Dayna yelled.

Shane and Brady plunged through the deep sand. Shane gripped Champagne's bridle. Brady grabbed Mystery's lead rope. "I've got him, Liv!" Brady hollered. "I'll try to hold him."

As she started toward Brady, Liv felt Mark tug on her sleeve. "We're like rats in a trap down here," he yelled. "We need to split up before the sandstorm blows itself out." He thrust Cisco's rope into Liv's hands and started up the side of the gulch without a backward glance.

"Wait! I'm coming with you." Sophie scrambled after her brother.

Liv watched them disappear into the screen of blowing sand. Was Mark trying to get away? It wouldn't work. The men at the top of the gulch would be able to see them as soon as the sandstorm moved on. Already, the howl of the wind was dying, the darkness dissipating.

❊ ❊ ❊ ❊ ❊

Sophie and Mark crawled over the edge of the gully on the far side of the coyotes' trailer. Keeping low to the ground, hidden by streamers of sand, they crept closer. The truck was stopped with its engine running. Its headlights threw an eerie glow through the red dust.

Sophie gripped Mark's hand. "What are we going to do?" she choked out the question.

Mark stared at the truck. "Maybe the guys will get out when the storm dies down a bit more." He pointed to the truck door. "And maybe they'll leave the truck running."

❊ ❊ ❊ ❊ ❊

"You're coming home with us," Liv stroked Mystery's black hide, now caked with dust. "You'll be safe."

Mystery's head shot up, throwing her backwards. Teeth bared, he whinnied his fury. In the next instant, Liv heard truck doors slam. "*Gracias, amigos*," the English-speaking man sang out. "We thank you for capturing our stallion once again. This time, we will take him from you."

Liv turned to see the coyote sliding down the side of the gulch, a wide grin on his face, arms stretched out for Mystery.

Before he could grab the rope out of her hands, fast as lightning Liv slipped the halter off Mystery's head. "GO!" she shouted with all her strength. "Get away – as far as you can. GO!"

She caught a flash from Mystery's wide intelligent eye as he reared, plunged, and took off down the gulch like a black rocket. In that flash was recognition, memory and knowledge. She knew Mystery would recognize her if they ever met again. Right now he was free, and that was what mattered.

"What have you done?" The coyote sputtered in fury. His partner spat a stream of Spanish at Liv that she was glad she could not understand.

"I'd rather lose him than let you have him." Liv faced the man, equally furious.

"I'll get you for this!" He lunged forward.

A sudden roar made the man spin away from her. Liv looked up to see the coyotes' truck heading for the edge of the gulch – Mark and Sophie leaping out the open doors on either side.

"*Eh tu! Camion! Parar!* Stop!" The two men scrambled to rescue their rig.

Sophie and Mark slid speedily down to the others. "Quick, get on the horses," Sophie shouted as they came.

Liv plunged back to Cactus Jack. "Come on, big guy," she told him as she hurled herself on his back. "Follow Mystery. He knows the way out of here."

She reached out a hand to help Brady up behind her, and glanced back to make sure the others were mounted. She saw the coyotes struggling to push the truck from below. The dirty old horse trailer held the pickup from pitching into the gulch. Its front end and hitch were high off the ground. "I don't think that rig is going anywhere," Liv yelled behind to Sophie. "They're stranded! Ya-hoo!"

She gave Cactus Jack a free rein. The deep sand at the bottom of the gulch made running hard at first, but soon the three horses hit firmer ground and the thud of their hoofs was a welcome sound, taking them farther and farther away from the coyotes.

Once they were far enough to feel safe they stopped for a drink, and shared the last of the water in their canteens with the weary horses. The sandstorm had moved on to the south. To the west, the sun was low in the sky like a glowing log in a bed of red-hot coals. Liv shivered. The sun might look hot, but the desert was cooling fast.

"You were so-o brave!" She hugged Sophie. "What made you think of taking the truck?"

"It was Mark's idea," Sophie explained. "He knew the guys would have to get out to come after the stallion."

"I saw it in a video game," Mark said with a grin. "Cool game – Avengers Revenge."

"What happened to their gun?" Brady asked. He put his arm around Liv to keep her from shivering.

"I threw it into the sand where they'll have a hard time finding it," Mark told him. "I thought of that idea myself."

"You did good," Shane said with a nod in Mark's direction. That was all, but Sophie and Liv shared a relieved glance. From shy, quiet Shane, that was high praise, and Mark seemed to know it. He nodded back.

They rode on. The gulch grew shallower when they reached the flat desert floor. Fifteen minutes later they came to the road, where they met a white truck driving slowly. "That's border patrol," Shane said, signaling the truck to stop.

"Are you kids from the Silver Spur ranch, by any chance?" an officer leaned out his window to ask as they dismounted. "We had a report that the Silver Spur rig was up there." He pointed to the Ocotillo Hills behind them. "A helicopter pilot named Hank called just before the sandstorm hit. We contacted your folks. They're worried, so call them, pronto."

"We lost our phone," Liv said. "Could we use yours?"

"Call your mom first," Dayna begged. "I'd rather not talk to my father. Wait till he hears about his truck!"

They made their calls. When Brady called home, Liv heard him say, "Six of us are out here with three tired horses." He leaned into the patrol truck. "Exactly where are we, sir?"

The patrol officer told him.

"We're six miles from the junction on Manzanita Road," Brady went back to speaking to his father. "If you could bring us a trailer, with some water for the horses ..."

"And for us!" Dayna shot in. "We look like a bunch of bush rats."

"I wasn't going to mention it," the officer said, "but you kids look like you were dragged through that sandstorm by a pack of coyotes."

Brady grinned, finished the conversation, and handed the phone back to the officer. "Thanks," he said. "Dad's coming to get us with the trailer. The horses can rest."

Liv sighed gratefully. Brady could be counted on when things got rough. There was one more thing she had to take care of. "Speaking of coyotes," she said to the patrol officer, "we met a couple of the human kind back there. Last we saw them they were trying to get their rig off the edge of a gulch."

The officer at the wheel put the truck in gear. "We've been looking for those boys," he said with a brisk nod. "Got another message from a horse trainer name of Buck Barnes, saying they might be around here." He gave one last look at the battered bunch. "Now you kids stay put, and when that trailer gets here, I want you to go *straight home*."

Six heads nodded wearily. This time, they would.

The patrol truck zoomed away. "I hope they get the coyotes." Liv looked after it and shook her fist. "Mystery won't be safe till those men are locked up or gone." Her face fell. "Even then, he won't be *really* safe. When I think how close we came to having him, I could cry!"

Sophie threw her arms around Cisco's neck. "*This* horse is my hero. He took care of Mark for me."

"Both our horses were strong, and brave and fabulous," Liv agreed, straightening Cactus Jack's dusty mane. "Granddad would be proud of them."

"But we're not going to tell him everything that happened, are we?" Dayna frowned. "Because the less my father knows about this little adventure, the better!"

CHAPTER 20
Changes

"We promised Dayna we wouldn't tell what happened yesterday, but it's a hard promise to keep." Sophie sighed as she brushed Cisco in the barn the next morning. "Everything feels different. For instance, how are we going to explain the way Mark suddenly decided to ride?"

"If anyone asks, say it was at the clinic in Fort Parson." Liv circled her currycomb along Cactus Jack's side. "Mark watched Buck Barnes train. He learned a lot so it's not totally a lie."

"I just wish Granddad could have seen how brave Mark was, riding after the coyotes' truck, and driving it over the edge of the gulch." Sophie waved her brush in the air. "Our brother was amazing, even though Cisco did a lot to make him look good. Didn't you, boy?" She scrubbed the spot between Cisco's ears where he liked to be rubbed.

Liv swung around at the sound of footsteps. "Here's Mark and Shane."

As usual, Shane had arrived before breakfast to work at the ranch. Liv and Sophie tried not to stare or giggle as the two boys walked into the barn. Mark was a mirror image of Shane – same wide-brimmed hat, striped shirt, lean denim jeans instead of his baggy black pants, leather chaps and boots. He even wore a belt with a silver buckle.

"Where did you …?" Liv started to ask, her eyes wide.

"No comments, little sisters." Mark tugged on his hat. "I borrowed this stuff from Shane. I thought I'd help him out around the ranch today. See how it goes."

"All right!" Liv was breathless.

At that moment Ted Starr strode into the barn, gave Mark one surprised glance, cleared his throat and asked, "How are the horses after yesterday?"

"They're fine, Granddad," Liv assured him. "You know how tough Cisco and Cactus Jack are."

"That's good. While it's still cool I'd like you girls and Shane to take a quick ride out to Wild Horse Creek Canyon. Check on Diego and the herd – see how they made out in the storm."

"We'll need another horse, Granddad," said Sophie, glowing. "Mark will probably want to go with us." *A short ride to the canyon will be perfect for him*! she thought.

"Oh?" Ted paused. "Is that true, Mark?" He looked like the hawk on the fencepost as he focused on his grandson.

"Yes, sir." Mark straightened his shoulders.

"That's fine, then. You can take Trixie." Ted Starr's hawk-like look softened and his blue eyes sparkled. "I guess you'll be wanting a driving lesson in my truck when you get back. We had a deal, remember?"

"I remember, Granddad." Mark smiled. "But there's no hurry – when you have time."

"Fine," Ted Starr repeated as he marched stiffly away. *As if it was the most natural thing in the world that Mark's riding with us*, Sophie thought happily. *As if he wasn't bursting with pride.*

✳ ✳ ✳ ✳ ✳

As they were about to leave, Dayna screeched to a stop in the ranch yard. She was driving her mother's white sports car.

"Hey!" She whipped off her sunglasses. "Mark! You look so great in normal clothes."

Mark grinned. The cowboy outfit was anything but normal to him, but he wasn't going to say that to Dayna. He sauntered up to the car as if he'd been wearing cowboy boots all his life. "What happened about your pickup?" he asked. "Was your father mad?"

"MAD?" Dayna laughed bitterly. "His face turned red and he stamped and snorted like an angry bull. I told him it wasn't my fault the truck broke down, or that some jerks came along and used the tires for target practice."

"But how did you explain being up in the Ocotillo Hills?" Sophie asked.

"I blamed it on Liv." Dayna shrugged. "I told him she insisted on searching for wild horses. He believed me – he knows she's a little bit *loca* herself."

"Thanks!" Liv exclaimed. *But I don't care what Sam Regis thinks of me*, she thought.

"I just came to see how you're all doin'." Dayna waved at their saddled horses. "But I can see you're ready to head out. Why don't we get together at my place tonight and celebrate our escape from the sandstorm – and other stuff. Shane can drive you." She shoved her sunglasses back on and backed the car up. "I'll pick up Brady. See you around seven!"

✳ ✳ ✳ ✳ ✳

As Mark and Sophie rode along the desert track from the ranch to Wild Horse Creek Canyon, Mark chatted to Cisco as if he and the sorrel horse were old friends. Sophie was riding the bay mare, Trixie, who seemed happy to be back on the herd's home ground. She whickered and blew and bobbed her head in pleasure.

Shane and Liv rode behind. Shane on his paint horse, Navajo, Liv on Cactus Jack. Tux, Shane's border collie, trotted alongside. "Mark looks pretty good on a horse now," Shane nodded ahead. "It seems Sophie's a better riding teacher than you are."

"Don't tease," Liv begged. "I can't take it this morning. I'm hoping like crazy that the canyon is so beautiful that it convinces Mark he wants to stay on the ranch."

"You might be dreamin'." Shane shook his head. "After yesterday, what with scorpions and horse smugglers and a sandstorm and all, Mark might just want to get out of here."

"It could go either way," Liv agreed. "But I feel like we changed in that sandstorm, like it scraped more than the skin of our faces. Look how close it brought Sophie and Mark." She sighed, watching her brother and sister riding side by side. "All I know is, today's ride might decide our whole future."

Their horses' hoofs clattered over the rocky trail that led deeper into the canyon. Mark stared in amazement as Liv caught up to him on Cactus Jack. "There are trees here," he said, "and it's green."

"Isn't it fantastic? There's a spring, just ahead around that bend," Liv sailed headfirst into her sales pitch. "It's the best water in this whole part of the desert. That's why Dayna's dad, Sam Regis, is so anxious to get his hands on the Lucky Star ranch. That's why we have to stay to protect it. We're the future of the ranch, you and Sophie and I!"

"And Shane," Sophie said softly. She wished her sister didn't always sound so sure and passionate about everything. It didn't give Mark a chance to make up his own mind.

Liv rushed on, her words tumbling over each other. "After it rains there is water in that stream." She pointed to a dry bed of smooth round boulders. "You should see it! And right there, standing on that dome of rock, is

146

where I first saw Mystery. He was so proud and beautiful. I'll never forget it."

"You forget that he fought with Diego and hurt him badly," Sophie couldn't resist shooting in. "If Mystery came back, they'd fight again and Diego might be killed."

"It doesn't have to happen that way." Liv shook her head firmly and straightened her shoulders. "Anyway, I'm going to keep searching for him. I feel like Mystery belongs to me, to us."

✳ ✳ ✳ ✳ ✳

They rode around the bend and there was the spring.

"That's the Lucky Star herd." Liv swept her arm around the scene. A small herd of horses grazed on the green grass at the edge of a watering hole. The steel-gray stallion, Diego, whinnied a greeting, and Bando the colt, in a comical imitation of his father, did the same. The other mares and foals went on munching peacefully.

"Great-looking horses!" Mark whistled. "Are they all ours?"

"Yes, and there used to be a lot more," Liv carried on. "Get Gran to tell you stories of how the first horses came to the ranch over a hundred years ago. She says Mom and you and I and Sophie have only been away for sixteen years. That's just a blink. Now we're home." She ran out of breath. "Mark! What do you think? Say something!"

CHAPTER 21
Party at the Silver Spur

"Well, what about it, Mark? Do you like our little spread?" Dayna looked up at him. She was sitting on the wall of a splashing fountain at her Silver Spur ranch, swinging her legs. Flowering bushes bloomed around her. Yellow lanterns flickered under the *ramada*, the woven roof of the patio.

"Yeah, it's pretty nice," Mark muttered.

It was clear to Liv, who was putting food on the patio table, that Mark liked the Silver Spur ranch a lot! Not only that, he liked Dayna. Liv recognized the look of hopeless longing on her brother's face. Dayna was as out of reach as the desert moon that soared above the ranch. She was not only a year older, she had a serious boyfriend.

She had seen that same longing look on Sophie's face when she looked at Shane. She had felt it herself when she thought about Mystery, the wild horse, now running far and free. They had been so close to rescuing him! *As for Brady*, she thought, *that isn't so hopeless. He might even ...*

"What are you thinking about?" Brady came up behind her so quietly she hadn't heard his step.

"Nothing special," she lied. "Just about the wild stallion, and how much Mark changed because of the sandstorm and everything that happened yesterday. I changed too – I know I'm only almost fourteen but I feel older."

"Do you think you're old enough for your first kiss?" Brady asked shyly.

"What? I ...uh..." Liv stammered. This wasn't what she was expecting! She always thought she'd have lots of time to get ready for her first real kiss. But Brady leaned toward her without waiting for her to put down the bowl in her hands. He didn't stumble, didn't trip or fall over anything. His lips brushed hers. It felt ... tingly, sweet, fizzy, wonderful!

"Wow!" said Liv and stepped back to gaze at Brady. "I think I got sour cream dip on your shirt."

"What's a little dip between friends?" Brady grinned. "*You* kissed *me* back. That's what matters." He took her hand. "What does it mean?"

"I don't know," Liv confessed, "but here comes Sophie with the guacamole!"

This was such a ridiculous thing to say in the circumstances that they both burst into giggles.

"What's so funny?" Sophie asked. She set down the bowl of green avocado dip and stared at them. "Do you two realize you're holding hands?"

"So we are!" Brady laughed. He swung their joined hands high in the air. "Let's go see if there's something else we can bring from the kitchen." He pulled Liv after him.

"I'll tell you later," Liv whispered to Sophie as they dashed away.

❋ ❋ ❋ ❋ ❋

Shane came to help Sophie under the *ramada*. "Where is everybody?" he asked.

"Brady and Liv are doing something in the kitchen." Sophie looked away from Shane's lean, handsome face. "Dayna and Mark seem to be getting along." She waved toward the two of them, still sitting on the fountain wall.

"Your brother was asking me about the high school." Shane took the forks from Sophie's hand and started placing them around the table. "Mark wanted to know about the sports, and the science program. He even wondered if I could teach him how to rope."

"You're putting those on the wrong side." Sophie took the forks back. "That sounds as if he's thinking we'll be here this fall," she said smiling. "Liv will be so excited!"